He could *dan*

The unexpected v
that first touch of
all on its own. Fin
disguise had been so shocking that part of her
brain had shut down. Her only thought had been
to finish the dance and escape.

Tony Grimshaw! The son of the city's mayor, no
less. The rising star of St. Pat's cardiothoracic
surgical team. Tipped to become the next head of
that prestigious department, despite being only in
his mid-thirties.

One of life's golden people. Only ever seen
accompanied by the wealthiest and most beautiful
women—often celebrities—and never encumbered
with small dependent children.

But he could dance. *Really* dance. And within
moments a forgotten joy was reborn for Kelly.

The spell they were under did odd things to the
passage of time. Kelly had no idea how long they
danced, and there was no way she was going to
suggest a break. The lights became dimmer and
the crowd on the dance floor thinned out, but still
they danced on.

As if there were no tomorrow.

Dear Reader,

A few years ago I did something I have always dreamed of doing—I started dancing lessons. I began with Ceroc, have dabbled with some swing, tango and hip-hop and am seriously trying ballroom at the moment. Salsa and jive are also on the list. I'm completely addicted. Not only is it the one physical activity I've discovered that is such fun you don't notice you're exercising, but when you dance with someone who really knows what he's doing, and you're floating around the floor to some gorgeous music, it's magic! Fairy-tale stuff.

What a perfect place to start a story. A fairy-tale kind of story with a heroine who's got it tough and a prince of a hero who's way out of her league. I had a ball—literally and figuratively! No glass slipper, but there is a substitute for a pumpkin coach and an almost–fairy godmother and even a frog. And there is definitely magic—the kind of magic that can happen in real life when two people who are meant to be together find each other and fall in love.

May a little fairy dust fall out from between the pages of this story and into *your* life!

Happy reading,

Alison

HOT-SHOT SURGEON, CINDERELLA BRIDE
Alison Roberts

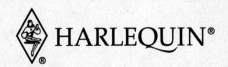

HARLEQUIN®

TORONTO • NEW YORK • LONDON
AMSTERDAM • PARIS • SYDNEY • HAMBURG
STOCKHOLM • ATHENS • TOKYO • MILAN • MADRID
PRAGUE • WARSAW • BUDAPEST • AUCKLAND

Recycling programs
for this product may
not exist in your area.

ISBN-13: 978-0-373-06695-7

HOT-SHOT SURGEON, CINDERELLA BRIDE

First North American Publication 2009

Copyright © 2009 by Alison Roberts

www.eHarlequin.com

Printed in U.S.A.

BILLIONAIRE DOCTORS

*Hot, jet-set docs at the top of their
game—professionally...and personally!*

These desirable doctors are international
playboys—gorgeous Greeks, sexy sheikhs,
irresistible Italians and Australian tycoons. Their
playground might be the world of the rich and
famous, but their professional reputations are
world renowned. These billionaires dedicate
themselves to saving lives by day—and red-hot
seduction by night....

CHAPTER ONE

WHO on earth was that?

The conversation he'd been engrossed in a moment ago became a meaningless blur of sound for Dr Anthony Grimshaw. For just a heartbeat he had caught a glimpse of the most stunning-looking woman he'd ever seen, standing between two pillars on the far side of the ballroom.

Much to the delight of the organising committee, St Patrick's fundraiser had become *the* function of the year, and there was a sea of people moving to the excellent music being provided by a small live orchestra. The dance floor was so well populated it was inevitable that his line of vision was obscured, but Tony still found himself trying to see those pillars again as he tuned back in to the voice beside him. A well respected voice that belonged to a senior colleague: paediatric cardiologist John Clifford.

'...and anyway, didn't I see a photo of you in some gossip rag? Out and about with Morrison's daughter? What's her name?'

'Miranda,' Tony supplied absently.

'Ah, yes! So. As I was saying. The fact that Gilbert's father is on the board should be well cancelled out by you having a prospective father-in-law with the same—if not greater—power to cast a vote in favour of *you* becoming HOD.'

'What?' Tony's attention was recaptured. 'What on earth are you talking about, John?'

'You. And Miranda.'

'There is no me and Miranda.'

'But…'

'We met at some charity do. Not unlike this one but without the fancy dress.' He smiled at the rotund figure of his companion. With his genial expression and fluffy mane of white hair it was no wonder his small patients loved him. Dr Clifford had answered tonight's medieval theme by wearing a king's robe and a crown. 'That outfit suits you, by the way. Very regal. Yes, Miranda and I went out a couple of times, but it's not going anywhere.'

'Why ever not? The girl's beautiful. Wealthy. Probably one of the many that seem to find you irresistible. My word, if I was still your age, I'd—'

The direct look Tony gave his companion was enough to break a flow that would have been extraordinary if they hadn't known each other so well for many years. In his early sixties, John Clifford was a family friend and had been Tony's mentor since he'd joined the staff of St Patrick's as a surgical registrar some years ago now.

'Don't you think it would seem a little blatant to

be dating the daughter of the chairman of St Pat's board of trustees at exactly the same time I'm up for the coveted position of head of the cardiothoracic surgical department?'

John's sigh was resigned. 'But it's the fact that you're young and single that counts against you, Tony. The powers-that-be see you as someone who's going to be distracted by a wife and family in the next few years. Responsibilities that might compromise your ability to lead the department into becoming the cutting-edge facility they've set their hearts on having.'

'I'll be able to assure them that isn't the case,' Tony said with quiet confidence. He tempered any implied criticism with a grin. 'With any luck Miranda will have told Daddy she broke it off with me because she wasn't about to try and compete with my job. That I'm far more interested in research than romance.'

The smile was returned. 'Don't understand it myself. She looked perfect.'

Tony's grin faded to a poignant curl. 'Want to know a secret, John?'

'What is it?'

Tony leaned closer. 'Perfection can be very, very boring.'

His gaze shifted as he straightened. Straight back to where he'd be able to see those pillars if the dancers would just move out of the way. His eyes narrowed as he tried to see past the colourful swirl of ornate costumes, and he only turned away briefly to acknowledge the farewell as John responded to a wave from another group.

What was it about that woman that drew his line of vision so compellingly? He was too far away to recognise her, or even see her features in the soft light from the flames of dozens of gas lamps on the walls of this vast ballroom. Maybe it was something about the way she was standing? Poised. Graceful even without any motion. With an aura that spoke of being alone but not lonely. Independent.

Yes, that was an intriguing enough impression to explain the attraction.

He felt a bit like that himself tonight. Independent. Free.

Part of it could be explained by the costume. Not that Tony had been keen on the idea of being one of the Three Musketeers when the idea had been mooted by one of his registrars, but much to his surprise he was loving it. The soft suede boots, tailored jacket, frilly shirt, and the sword dangling by his side. Even the wig and preposterously wide hat with its ridiculous feather. Not one to do anything by halves, he'd added a mask, moustache and neat goatee beard, which had the unexpected bonus of being a very effective disguise.

The rest of it could probably be attributed to the conversation he'd just been having with John. Or perhaps more to the ending of it. Not that he ever minded talking shop, but he was more than happy to forget the background tension of the career competition he was currently engaged in. He could probably avoid it for the rest of the evening, too, in this disguise. Now that he was alone he could virtually disappear into this incredibly colourful crowd, half of whom *he* wouldn't be able to recognise.

Like that woman between the pillars.

The princess with the dark dress and jewels sparkling in her hair.

He watched the crowd of dancers, enjoying the visual feast of this enormous costume party. The timeframe had been—loosely-adhered to, and the variety was impressive. There were knights and highwaymen, kings and queens and Vikings. Milkmaids and monks and jesters. Crusaders and pirates. More than one Merlin and a good crowd of peasants.

And…*yes*—there she was again!

Dancing, now. With a Robin Hood who was possibly a little merrier than he should be. Not the best dancer, in any case. But the princess…she was on another level entirely. The grace with which she had been holding herself whilst standing still had been a faint reflection of her body in movement.

The way she turned—with that subtle bend, like a leaf in a gentle breeze.

The way her hand traced a shape only she could feel in the air. The shape of the music as it danced in his ears.

There had to be a better position from which to watch the dance floor. One without the frustration of having his view constantly interrupted in this fashion. The best available seemed to be where *she* had been standing. Between those pillars.

Having chosen his desired position, Tony moved with a determination that had the customary effect of people unconsciously moving aside to clear his path.

Who on earth was *that?*

Standing there, at the vantage point she had recently vacated herself.

No—lounging might be a better word, with the padded shoulder of an ornate red jacket shifting his weight onto that pillar. On one foot with the other crossed elegantly at ankle level and just the toe of the boot touching the floor. Kelly almost expected to see him twirl the end of that fake moustache or sweep his hat off as she noticed him watching her.

Was he watching her?

Hard to tell with that mask and the flickering shadows from the atmospheric lighting behind the pillar, but it didn't matter because it *felt* as if he was watching her—and there was something incredibly exciting about the notion. Kelly wanted to be watched. To feel…desirable.

He was tall and lean. In a costume that could only be considered ideal fodder for a romantic fantasy. And that was precisely what Kelly was in the mood for.

This whole night was a fantasy as far as she was concerned. It had been ever since she had become the envied winner of the raffle for one of the astonishingly expensive tickets to St Patrick's annual ball. Not that she'd intended to actually come. That had

been Elsie's doing. Her boss. Surrogate mother, almost. It had been Elsie who'd hunted down the costume hire shops and dragged her along after work.

Even then Kelly had been ready to give her ticket away. She'd barely listened to Elsie clucking on about how much she was looking forward to baby-sitting Flipper. Or to the pointed reminders of how much she loved to dance.

'I dance every day,' she'd told Elsie. 'Flipper lives for her music.'

'Not the same as being in the arms of some tall, dark, handsome stranger, though, is it?'

'A man is the last thing I need in my life right now.'

She'd said it with the conviction of utmost sincerity. She'd just been jumping through hoops as she tried to find an acceptable excuse to decline. But then she'd seen the dress in the shop.

Midnight-blue velvet. High-waisted, with a laced bodice over a silver chemise. Sleeves that were shaped with a long, long back to them that would almost touch the ground. Folds of soft material that shimmered when she couldn't resist touching the garment.

It was a dress that could almost dance all by itself, and as her fingers had trailed down the skirt Kelly had known she was lost.

For just one night, she *had* to wear that dress.

And dance like there was no tomorrow.

Robin Hood was an unskilled but enthusiastic

dancer. It was easy to slip from his grasp and put some of her own style into the nondescript pattern they had been locked into. Kelly stepped back, raised her arms to cross them over her head, and, with her hands held like butterfly wings, she spun herself around fast enough to make the full folds of her dress billow. Then she caught the hand of her partner, twirled beneath it, and stepped back into his arms for some more sedate steps.

'Wow!' he said. 'Do it again.'

This time Kelly kept hold of Robin's hand and turned sideways before spinning in to lean on his shoulder. For just a split second before the spin her line of vision had those pillars directly ahead of her, and it was all too easy to imagine that *he* was watching her.

That he *wanted* her.

The orchestra was in no hurry to complete this particular medley, and suddenly neither was Kelly.

Poor Robin Hood was simply an accessory. She was dancing for *him*. The stranger in the shadows. Why him? she wondered fleetingly. There was something about the way he was standing there, she decided. The way he might be watching her, as though he found her attractive. But more, it was a vehicle for unleashing a side of herself that had been neglected for so long it was virtually forgotten.

The sensuous side.

Dancing would have been enough to satisfy her if she'd been with a partner who could have challenged her ability or let her express herself completely.

This fantasy of dancing to attract a total stranger was exciting enough to fill any gap this somewhat stilted movement left. The dress had already made Kelly feel beautiful. Being watched made it real.

She could dance her way into his heart.

Seduce him without touching. Without even seeming to notice him. And then she could melt into the crowd and simply disappear, to leave him wondering who the hell she was. The smile touching Kelly's lips was unconscious. It was a fitting part of this fairytale night. A bit of magic, like a tiny crystal ball she would be able to keep and look into occasionally when she wanted to remember feeling this good.

'Wow,' Robin Hood said again as the music finally faded. 'You're something else! What's your name?'

Kelly laughed. 'Cinderella.'

He grinned. 'Fair enough. Can I get you a glass of champagne, Cinders?'

'No—thank you.'

They both turned at the sound of the decisive negative, and Kelly felt a prickle run down her spine. How had he moved so fast? He must have been waiting for precisely this opportunity.

The musketeer swept a hand up in front of his chest and then moved it sideways in a graceful arc that left his fingers enticingly close to Kelly's.

'*My* dance, I think,' he said.

'Hang on, buddy!' Robin Hood was scowling. 'I was just going to get…'

Kelly could see, no—feel the commanding stare

her recent dance partner was receiving. In normal life that kind of arrogance would have put her back up instantly—but this wasn't normal life, was it? It was a fairytale, and *he* wanted to dance with her.

With a totally uncharacteristic, demure downward glance, Kelly put her hand into his.

The touch of her hand was like…like nothing Tony had ever felt before when his skin had come into contact with that of another person.

Thank goodness she took his hand when she did, because Tony had been experiencing an astonishingly strong desire to say something to Robin Hood that he might regret.

No one, *nothing*, was going to take away his chance to meet this woman. He tightened his grip around that slim hand.

What on earth was happening to him? The Grimshaws never behaved with anything less that the utmost decorum in public. He cast a suspicious glance at the cause of his unusual emotional state, but she was looking at the floor and standing very still in that poised manner she had. If Tony hadn't just spent nearly ten minutes watching her dance and finding his heart rate steadily increasing, his breathing becoming shallow and his tight breeches becoming less comfortable by the second, he might have believed her to be completely innocent.

Robin Hood muttered something unintelligible as he melted into the crowd, and it was only then that the princess raised her gaze. Tony was instantly aware of two things.

That they both knew their behaviour to her last dance partner had been unacceptably rude but also unavoidable. And that something was happening here that was simply meant to be.

Something as unreal as pretending to be part of a medieval gathering.

No. He'd better make that three things.

His awareness of this woman's beauty had been overwhelming even from the distance of the pillars. This close, Tony could believe he was looking at the nearest thing to perfection in a woman he'd ever seen.

Dark, dark blue eyes. Pale skin made all the more dramatic by the fall of that glorious wig. He'd been watching the black ripples that fell to her waist lift and swirl as she danced, and was thankful she hadn't braided it, or bundled it up to wear one of those pointy hats with veils attached at the sides that some women were wearing tonight. Dark stones like teardrops lay against her forehead, and the chain of jewels was the only restraint to her loose, flowing locks.

His hand lifted of its own accord to touch a soft curl.

'Nice,' he murmured. 'It feels almost real.'

'Does it?' A tiny smile pulled up the corners of her mouth and Tony found himself staring. Trying to extinguish what threatened to be an irresistible urge to kiss her.

Right here. Right now. In the middle of a dance floor where people around them had already started to dance to a new bracket of songs. Slightly faster music at the moment. Like his heartbeat.

'Shall we?' He gave a mock bow. Play-acting seemed to be the way forward here, because none of this felt real.

'Please.' The smile had an impish quality. 'But…'

'But?'

'I'm just wondering how safe it is to dance with you.'

Oh, not safe at all, he thought, but he pressed his lips closed on the warning and raised his eyebrows instead.

'Your sword?'

'Oh…' With a slow, deliberate, one-handed movement, Tony unbuckled the big silver clasp and pulled the belt from his waist. He looked up to inform the princess of his plan to drop the accessory out of the way—by the pillars, perhaps, along with his hat.

She looked up at the same instant, from where she had clearly been staring at his hands, and when he saw the tip of her tongue emerge to run across her bottom lip it felt as if some giant vice was squeezing every last molecule of oxygen from his chest.

Yes!

She wanted him. The way he wanted her.

Desire threatened to suffocate him. He could simply walk out of this ballroom and take her somewhere more private, couldn't he? No. It was a long time since he'd been an inexperienced teenager, for whom where lust could obliterate the ability to think clearly. This combination of confidence and anticipation might be heady stuff, but experience had taught him something else as well. It was a thrill that should be savoured for as long as possible.

Somehow he sucked in a breath as he led her to the edge of the floor to get rid of his unwanted accessories. Then he drew her into his arms.

'Did I hear correctly?' he enquired politely. 'Is your name Cindy?'

Those eyes were huge and... Dear Lord, even the way she blinked so slowly was erotic.

'Yes,' she said softly.

'Cindy who?'

'Does it matter?'

'It might.'

He could feel her responsiveness as he manoeuvred them to a clear space on the floor. She felt weightless in his arms, like an extension of his own body rather than a separate partner. God, if she felt like this on a dance floor, what would she be like in *bed?*

He saw the way the soft mounds of her breasts, pushed up by the corset top of her dress, rose even further as she took a deep breath. His mouth went dry.

'Riley,' she said at last. 'My name is Cindy Riley.'

'And you work at the hospital, Cindy Riley?'

'Yes.'

'Whereabouts? Which department?'

'All over.' She was smiling again. 'A bit of everything, really.'

Ah... She must be a pool nurse. Filling in wherever they required assistance. No wonder he hadn't seen her often enough in one place to recognise her. Tony ignored the scoffing sound in the back of his mind. The voice that said he would have only needed to see her once to recognise her again.

'Favourite places?'

'Emergency,' she said without hesitation. He could see the flicker in her eyes that spoke of a real passion for her work. 'And Theatre.'

Tony pulled her a little closer. 'My kind of girl,' he told her. 'And my favourite places as well. I'm Tony Grimshaw, by the way. I'm on the cardiothoracic surgical team.'

'Mmm.' The sound seemed oddly strangled. 'Could we stop talking, please, Tony Grimshaw? And dance?'

By way of response, Tony altered the way he was holding her. He might be rusty, but already the short time of moving with this woman felt natural. He sent Cindy Riley into a brief spin and then caught her, stepping sideways so that she could bend and dip— one arm extending gracefully. Then, the instant she was back on balance, he flipped her into a dip on his other side.

She was laughing as she came upright again, those incredible eyes letting him know that she was happy.

Impressed.

That she wanted more.

CHAPTER TWO

HE COULD *dance*!

The unexpected way her body had responded to that first touch of their hands had been disturbing all on its own.

Finding out who was beneath that disguise had been so shocking part of her brain had shut down, and her only thought had been to finish this dance and escape.

Tony Grimshaw! The son of the city's mayor, no less. The rising star of St Pat's cardiothoracic surgical team. Tipped to become the next head of that prestigious department, despite being only in his mid-thirties.

One of life's golden people. Only ever seen to be accompanied by the cream of available women. The wealthiest and most beautiful. Often celebrities, and never encumbered with small dependent children.

Criteria Kelly could never aspire to attaining. Wouldn't want to, in fact.

But he could dance. *Really* dance. And within moments a forgotten joy was reborn for Kelly.

Like flying. Taking off and swooping and knowing it was perfectly safe because there were strong arms to catch her. A lead that not only provided an impressive variety of moves but one that encouraged independence and gave opportunities to play.

Escape was the last thing she wanted now, and the music fading at the end of the set would have been utterly disappointing except that it went virtually unnoticed. The only change was that Tony slowed down. Held her close and started a tango step. And Kelly could rest her head against his and keep her eyes closed and still think of nothing but the music and the way they moved together so beautifully.

It didn't matter now that she was dancing with the physical embodiment of everything she had run from in her previous life. Or that she had lied about her identity.

It wasn't really a lie, was it?

Cindy Riley was close enough to being Cinderella to be a joke. Part of the pretence. Part of the fairytale she was living tonight. And it was…magic.

The spell they were under did odd things to the passage of time. Kelly had no idea how long they danced, and there was no way she was going to suggest a break. That would come all too soon—when the clock struck midnight and she had to flee. The lights became dimmer and the crowd on the dance floor thinned out, but still they danced on.

As if there was no tomorrow.

And maybe the spell was going to last a little longer than midnight.

At some point, drugged by the music and the movement, and barely moving in the slow, slow tango, she heard Tony murmur in her ear.

'I want to be with you,' he said. 'Somewhere else.'

She hadn't expected this. The thought was alarming. 'T-tonight?'

'Oh, yes.' The movement of his hand on her back was subtle. Nobody else would have noticed the way his thumb moved and pressed down along the bumps of her spine. But Kelly could feel the heat spread through her entire body. Into every single cell.

His voice was such a low rumble that Kelly felt rather than heard the two words he added.

'*All* night.'

His lips were right beside her ear. She felt them move like a caress. She felt the tiny coolness of his tongue touching her skin.

Yes!

No!

It was unthinkable! To spend a night with a man she'd just met for the first time? Not even met him honestly, come to that, seeing as he had no idea who she really was.

But maybe that made it less shocking somehow—because it wasn't *her* doing something so risky. So unlike anything she'd ever contemplated doing. She wasn't herself. Wasn't expected to be until around eight tomorrow morning, when she was due to collect Flipper from Elsie's house. Just for tonight— a few more hours—she could continue being part of the fairytale and do things she might never get the chance to do again.

She could believe she was someone that a man like Tony actually wanted.

'Wh—where?' she heard herself whisper.

'The owners of this hotel are family friends. I have a suite upstairs for the night.'

His head was moving as he spoke. His lips brushing her cheek. Any moment now and he might kiss her, and—God help her—Kelly wanted him to. She wanted the touch of his lips more than she had ever wanted anything.

Ever.

It was too easy. Kelly was being led as decisively as he had been leading her in their dancing. Doubts collided in her mind, but wouldn't slow down enough to take shape. Not when he was looking down at her like this and she could see the dark eyes behind the mask.

'Don't worry,' he said softly. 'You're safe. I'll take care of you, Cindy Riley. I promise.'

And that was her undoing.

The thought of being cared for.

Loved.

It wasn't the first time Tony Grimshaw had taken a woman he barely knew to his bed. The only difference between his testosterone-laden teen years and those of most young men had been the playground he'd had available. One where the kind of holidays, clothes, cars and freedom had been a magnet for every pretty girl he'd encountered.

So why did it feel like the first time?

Tony led Cindy through the door of the best suite the Grand Chancellor had to offer, pushed it closed with his foot and pulled her into his arms, dipping his head to claim her lips with his own as part of the same, fluid series of moves.

It was all just another kind of dance, really, wasn't it? And he'd been right. Her responsiveness was… mind-blowing. The way her mouth moved under his and her lips parted. They way her tongue touched and curled against his own. And when he moved his head to deepen the kiss she tilted her own to exactly the angle he needed to explore her delicious mouth a little more thoroughly.

It was some time before he registered what his fingers, rather than his lips and tongue, were aware of.

'Your hair,' he said in amazement. 'It's *real*.'

She laughed. 'Of course it is.'

He smiled back at her. He wanted to make her laugh again because it was such a gorgeous sound. 'Mine isn't.'

It worked. 'I should hope not.' Then her face stilled. 'Take it off,' she whispered. 'I want to feel *you*. Take off the wig. And this—' She touched the moustache that was already half detached after their kisses.

She didn't seem to mind that his own hair was flattened and damp from the wig. Or that his chin felt rough because he hadn't shaved before sticking on that silly beard. Her hands shaped his head, and the pressure brought his lips back to hers for an even more intense kiss.

Tony had to slow things down. He wanted her right now. To pull up the acres of fabric in that dress and take her here, against the wall. But he'd promised to take care of her, hadn't he? And even if he hadn't made that promise, he wouldn't want to rush this. It was too special.

He dragged his mouth from hers, but he couldn't pull right back. He kissed the corner of her mouth. Then her jaw and her neck. She tilted her head back in response to his touch, and the gasp as he trailed his kisses down to the pale flesh rounded over the top of her corset made him utter a sound that was unfamiliar to his own ears.

A primal sound of pure need.

His fingers fumbled with the string at the front of her bodice and then her hands joined his, making deft, sure movements that undid the knot and loosened the lace. And all the time her fingers worked under his, her eyes held his gaze. Tony thought he was going to drown in the deep blue depths. In the desire he could see that so clearly matched his own.

Then the laces were undone and her breasts were free and his hands could hold them and he could bend his head and touch his tongue to nipples as hard as buttons.

And he was lost.

Completely and utterly lost.

Kelly wasn't a virgin, but it had been a very long time since she'd been with a man—and she'd never been with anyone as far out of her league as Tony Grimshaw.

Maybe that was why it felt like a first time.

Or maybe it was because *this* man made her feel different. Every touch made her ache for more, but even the combination of long abstinence on her part and gentleness and strength on his part, overlying the undeniable expertise of his lovemaking, couldn't explain why this felt so different.

He seemed to know her body. Just where to touch her and *how*. With his lips, his tongue, his teeth. His hands and his fingertips. His *eyes*! The way he looked at her body as he uncovered it. The way he held her gaze as he stripped off his own clothing.

And his focus. He'd stopped talking and asking awkward questions when she had wanted to dance, and now there seemed no need for any words at all. With the costumes that represented the first chapters of this fairytale lying puddled on the floor, Tony scooped Kelly into his arms and carried her to the massive bed, softly illuminated by discreet lamps.

He laid her down, took a condom from the drawer in the bedside cabinet and then knelt over her on the bed.

There was no going back now. Even if escape had

been offered, Kelly would have been totally unable to accept. She looked at the beautiful body of the man she was with. The hard lines of muscle. The faint smudges of dark hair. The *size* of him in more ways than the obvious. Because Kelly could sense his generosity of spirit. His ability to care.

That recognition took her breath away.

She was completely lost. She held up her arms to welcome him, but he didn't return her faintly tentative smile. His face was so serious, so *intent*, she experienced a moment of fear that made her heart stop and then thump painfully hard.

He caught her wrists and lowered her arms until he was holding them, crossed over her head. He transferred both wrists easily to one hand and then, as he bent his mouth to hers, his free hand slipped the curtain of her long hair from where it covered her breast. Gentle fingers traced her neck, along her collarbone, and then dipped to come up from beneath her breast and skim her nipple.

The shaft of exquisite sensation made Kelly gasp, and he raised his mouth from hers, releasing her wrists and using both hands to touch her as his lips took over from his fingers on her breast. But only for a heartbeat. His mouth kept moving, his tongue finding her belly button and then leaving a line of fire as it tracked further down.

She left her arms where they were, above her head, and lay still for as long as possible. But with the first sweep of his tongue on that tiny nub of hidden flesh she came—with a shudder and a groan of disbelief. She had to touch him then. To try and give back some of the magic that was dusting this incredible night.

She cried out again later, when he finally entered her and they began a whole new dance. And when she held him after his own shuddering climax she could feel the same kind of wonder emanating from him. And it felt as if she was touching his soul.

It was a night she never wanted to end, but of course it had to.

The magic was fading when Tony finally fell asleep, one arm flung above his head, the other holding Kelly close to his side. But the luxury of falling asleep and then waking to make love yet again was one Kelly couldn't afford. With the first fingers of light reaching into the velvety darkness in the corners of the room, she eased herself from the bed so stealthily that Tony did nothing more than take a deeper breath.

She put the dress back on, but its magic had also evaporated and Kelly could feel reality kicking in. It felt wrong to be dressed like this.

Wrong to have just spent a night having the most astonishingly wonderful sex imaginable?

No.

Kelly took one last, long look at the man sprawled on the bed, deeply asleep.

Something that had felt so right couldn't be wrong.

Softly, she kissed her fingertips and blew the kiss towards the man who still didn't know who she was.

Or anything about the life she was about to step back into.

And that was the way it had to be.

The truth would only tarnish the fairytale, and Kelly wanted to keep it exactly the way it was.

Perfect.

CHAPTER THREE

'You're in luck, Kelly, love. They're short in ED today.'

'Cool. Thanks, Elsie.' Kelly was still tucking the long coil of her braid under the elastic band of the oversized shower-cap-type hat that was part of her uniform. 'For the whole shift?'

'Yep.' Elsie was giving her a curious look. 'I thought you'd be rapt. Isn't Emergency your favourite place?'

'It is.' Kelly nodded and smiled, but her brain had gone into overdrive.

No wonder Elsie had picked up on something being different. Only last week the prospect of a day in the emergency department would have been a treat.

A poignant treat, mind you—it was like having her face pressed to a shop window that contained something ultimately desirable but equally unaffordable—but still an irresistible one.

'I'm just a bit tired,' she told Elsie, by way of

excusing her lack of excitement. 'I didn't sleep very well.'

'Are you OK?'

'I'm fine.' Kelly's smile was wider this time. Physically, the only thing that had disturbed her rest was the pleasure of experiencing the delicious tingles her body could conjure up with remarkable ease as she remembered the night with her musketeer. 'Maybe I just had too much excitement the night before.'

'Hmm.' Elsie looked unconvinced. 'You haven't said much about that. You did have a good time, then?'

'Magic,' Kelly affirmed.

So fabulous she couldn't begin to try describing it. And she didn't want to, despite sensing that Elsie felt left out and maybe a little hurt.

'I only went because of you,' she added. 'Thank you so much!'

It had been a night of pure magic. One that she intended to treasure for the rest of her life. And that was where the problem now lay. The repercussions that were going to affect a very large part of her life.

Reality couldn't be allowed to intrude, because she knew without a shadow of a doubt that reality would tarnish, if not completely destroy, the joy of that magic. That was why she needed to keep it private, and not diminish its perfection by talking about it. It was also why the dreadful prospect of Tony Grimshaw recognising her at work had made sleep so elusive.

'Is Flipper all right?' Briefly mollified, Elsie was now frowning anxiously. 'I did wonder if she had a bit of a sniffle on Saturday night. I noticed she was breathless going up my stairs.'

'Was she?' Kelly caught her bottom lip between her teeth, her mind whirling in a new direction. 'I'll mention it to Dr Clifford. She's got a check-up scheduled for this week.'

'But she's not sick today?'

'No. She couldn't wait to get to crèche. As usual.'

'What day's her appointment?'

'Wednesday. Sorry, Elsie. I forgot to say I wouldn't be working.'

'Not a problem. That's why I keep you on the casual list and why you get sent all over the show. Speaking of which—' Elsie glanced at her watch '—it's seven-thirty already. They will have finished hand-over.'

'I'm gone.' Kelly stood on one foot and then the other to pull disposable shoe-covers over her old, comfortable trainers.

'Report to the nurse manager when you get there. I'm not sure if they need you out front or in the observation area.'

Kelly took the shortcut of some fire escape stairs, as familiar with the layout of this vast hospital as she was with her own home. It was a world of its own in here, and she loved it despite the fact that her dream had never had her working in quite this capacity.

'Hey, Tom!' Kelly gave a cheerful wave to an orderly pushing an empty wheelchair in the opposite direction. Then she turned abruptly and chose a different direction when she saw the group of doctors coming behind Tom. She could take another route to the emergency department. She could use the service elevator and avoid any risk of recognition.

At least her uniform should be an effective disguise. The shower cap, the shapeless pink smock and the shoe-covers. Almost the same uniform the cleaners and kitchen staff wore—because, as a nurse aide, Kelly was part of the faceless army of people whose ranks stretched from groundsmen to technicians and kept this busy city hospital functioning the way it should. Making up the dark sky that allowed stars like Tony Grimshaw to shine so brightly.

Emergency should be safe enough, Kelly reassured herself as she sped down the final corridor, past the pharmacy and gift shop. It was rare for someone other than a registrar to make an initial assessment of a need for surgery. Being around the cardiology wards or theatre suites might be another matter, however. Kelly would need to stay on guard.

Not that she was likely to forget any time soon. Not when he was still in her head to this degree. When just a flicker of memory made her want to smile. Forgetting it enough to focus on her job might prove to be a problem, but it soon became apparent that her concern—for the moment, at least—was groundless.

The department was busy enough to keep her completely focussed. Fetching and carrying supplies, taking patients to the toilet or supplying bedpans,

dealing with vomit containers and spills on the floor.
She'd worked here often enough to be familiar with
everything she needed to know. Many of the staff
recognised her. One nurse looked particularly
pleased to see her when she took a fresh linen bag
to hang in the main resuscitation area.

'Kelly! Just the person I need. You know where
everything is around here, don't you?'

'Pretty much.'

'Help me sort out this mess?' The wave indicated
a benchtop littered with supplies that hadn't been put
away. 'We've got an MVA victim coming in, and if
it's still looking like this when they arrive, my guts
will be someone's garters.'

It was fun, working under pressure. Handling
syringes and bags of saline and packages containing
endotracheal tubes. Things that had once been so
familiar. Part of the dream Kelly had been well on
her way to attaining.

'Want any sizes smaller than a seven on the tray?'
she asked the nurse. 'Do you know what's coming
in?'

'Something major.'

More staff were beginning to assemble in the
room.

'Where's Radiology?' someone called. 'And the
surgical reg—is she on her way?'

'I'd better get out of here,' Kelly said.

'No! Look!'

Kelly looked. Cupboard doors were open below
the bench, with supplies spilling into a heap on the

floor. They encroached over the red line on the floor that was there to keep unnecessary personnel from the area around a patient. Right at the head of the bed, too, where the person responsible for the patient's airway would be in danger of tripping over them.

Swiftly, Kelly crouched and began to stack the awkward packages back into the cupboards, so focussed on doing it as quickly as possible she barely registered the increasing level of activity behind her.

And then suddenly the double doors were pushed open and controlled chaos ensued.

'Seventeen-year-old, pushbike versus truck,' a paramedic informed the receiving doctor. 'Handlebar of the bike penetrated the left side of his chest. Intubated on scene and decompression attempted for a tension pneumothorax. Oxygen saturation's currently—'

Kelly was rising slowly to her feet, her back to the bench, and she slid sideways to get out of the way, horrified at being somewhere she had no right to be. Her gaze was none the less fixed on the scene so close to her. The transfer of the patient from the ambulance stretcher to the bed.

'On the count of three. One…two…*three!*'

There was a reassessment of all the vital signs, like heart-rate and blood pressure and respiration rate. None of them was looking good. Monitors were being hooked up and requests being called for more equipment and extra personnel. No one had time to notice Kelly, still standing in the corner.

She knew she had to leave. There was no way a nurse's aide could be any use at all in the kind of life-and-death drama about to be played out in here.

Bags of intravenous fluids were being clipped to overhead hooks. The doctor in charge of the airway was bag-masking the teenage boy, his eyes on the monitor screen that was showing him how much oxygen they were getting into his circulation. He didn't look happy with the figures he could see.

'Saturation's dropping. We're below ninety percent. And what the hell's happened to that ECG?'

An electrode had been displaced while moving the boy from the stretcher to the bed. Nursing staff were busy cutting away clothing and hadn't noticed the lead dangling uselessly, tangled up with the curly cord of the blood pressure cuff.

Without thinking, Kelly stepped forward into a gap, untangled the lead, and clipped the end back to the sticky pad attached beneath the patient's right collarbone.

'Thanks.' The doctor hadn't taken his eyes off the monitor, and Kelly could see why. The trace now travelling across the screen was erratic, and the unusual shapes of the spiky complexes suggested that this young boy was in imminent danger of a cardiac arrest.

Another doctor had his stethoscope on the less injured side of the chest. Was it proving too hard for one lung to function well enough to sustain life? Was the heart itself badly injured? Or was this boy simply bleeding too badly from internal injuries to make saving his life an impossibility?

Kelly was back in her corner. Transfixed. She could feel the tension rising with every second that ticked relentlessly past. With every command from the emergency department specialists, who were finding it difficult to gain extra IV access and infuse the blood volume that was so desperately needed, judging by the way the blood pressure was continuing to fall.

'Didn't someone page Cardiothoracic?' a doctor snapped. 'Where the hell are they?'

'Right here,' a calm voice responded. 'What are we dealing with?'

Kelly actually gasped aloud as Tony Grimshaw stepped closer to the bed, pulling on a pair of gloves. Not that there was the slightest danger of being noticed. At the precise moment the surgeon finished speaking, an alarm sounded on a monitor. And then another.

'VF,' someone called.

'No pulse,' another added.

'Start CPR.' The order came from the head of the bed. 'And charge the defibrillator to three-sixty.'

'Wait!' Tony's hands were on the patient's chest, lifting a blood-soaked dressing to examine the wound. 'Have you got a thoracotomy trolley set up?'

'Yes, I'll get it.' An ED registrar leaned closer. 'You're thinking tamponade? What about a needle pericardiocentesis first?'

'Wasting time,' Tony decreed. 'We're either dealing with a cardiac injury or major thoracic blood loss that needs controlling. Can I have some rapid skin preparation, please? We're not going to attempt full asepsis and draping, but I want everyone in here wearing a mask. And let's see if we can get a central line in while I'm scrubbing.'

Masks were tugged from the boxes attached to the wall as trolleys were moved and rapid preparation for the major intervention of opening the boy's chest continued. Kelly grabbed a mask for herself. A perfect disguise—just in case she got noticed when she made her move towards the exit.

Except she couldn't move. A thoracotomy for penetrating chest trauma topped the list for emergency department drama, and staff who had no more reason to be here than she were now finding excuses to slip into the back of the room to observe. House surgeons, registrars and nursing staff were squeezed into the space behind the red lines, and Kelly was trapped at the back. Able to hear everything, and even find a small window between the shoulders of the people directly in front of her, that afforded a good view of the surgeon if not the procedure.

He now had a hat and mask and gown over the Theatre scrubs he had been wearing on arrival. He seemed unconcerned by his audience. Ready to use an incredibly tense situation as a teaching tool, in fact.

'I'll use a "clam shell" approach,' he told the closest doctors. 'The one you guys would be using if I wasn't here.'

'Yeah…right,' someone near Kelly muttered. An over-awed medical student, perhaps?

She saw the flash of a scalpel being lifted from the sterile cover of the trolley.

'Bilateral incisions,' Tony said. 'About four centimetres in length, in the fifth intercostal space, mid-axillary line.'

Blood trickled down the yellow staining of hurriedly applied antiseptic on the boy's chest. Kelly was struck by how frail the young chest suddenly seemed.

'Make sure you breach the intercostal muscles and the parietal pleura. With a bit of luck we might deal with a tension pneumothorax and get some cardiac output at this point.'

They didn't.

Tony took just a moment to watch the screen, however, and his voice was soft. 'What's his name?'

'Michael.'

'And he's seventeen?'

'Yes.'

'Family here?'

'His mother's just arrived. She's in the relatives' room.'

Tony simply nodded, but Kelly was allowing herself to stare at him in the wake of his rapid-fire surprising queries. How had he done that? Made this seem so much more personal? As though he cared more about the patient than demonstrating his obviously not inconsiderable skills? Maybe he wasn't as hung up on his status as rumour had led her to believe.

She held her breath, watching the swift and decisive

actions of this surgeon as he used a fine wire saw to cut though the sternum and then opened the chest with retractors.

'I'm "tenting" the pericardium,' he said moments later. 'Scissors—thanks. Make a long incision like this. If it's too short, it'll prevent access to the heart. Suction…'

What would it be like, Kelly wondered, to have this man as a mentor in a career as a cardiothoracic surgeon? Or just to work alongside him as a nurse? To know him on a personal basis?

Maybe *she* knew him better than anyone else in this room.

A ridiculous thought, given the situation. Given reality. It made her memories of her time with him more dreamlike. Precious, but harder to hang onto. Kelly tucked them protectively into a corner of her mind.

Into that empty space in her heart.

Tony had both hands inside the boy's chest now, massaging Michael's heart. 'Make sure you keep the heart horizontal during massage,' he told the observers. 'Lifting the apex can prevent venous filling. I'm aiming for a rate of eighty per minute here, and I'm looking for any obvious bleeding that we need to control.'

The people in front of Kelly were murmuring in awed tones, and they shifted enough to obscure her line of vision. She heard the request for internal defibrillation, however, and could envisage the tiny paddles that would provide a minimal jolt to the cardiac tissue but hopefully restore a more normal heartbeat.

A collective gasp of amazement rippled around the room seconds later, but she could sense no let-up in control of a difficult situation from the star at the centre of this drama.

'Theatre's on standby. Let's get Michael up there while we've got a perfusing rhythm.'

There was a new flurry of activity as the open chest wound was covered, and the bed, the monitors and numerous necessary staff members all began moving as a connected unit.

Tony stripped off his gloves, dropping them to the floor and reaching for a fresh pair. His gaze scanned the assembled staff as he took a single step to put him within reach of what he needed. Kelly felt the eye contact like something physical. Almost a blow, the way it sent shock waves through her body. Despite the contact being so brief—less than a heartbeat—the connection was so strong she was sure Tony had to feel it, too. He'd glance back—with a frown, maybe. Needing a second glance without having registered why.

But he didn't look back. He barely broke his stride as he pulled fresh gloves from the slot on the box and followed his patient towards Theatre.

Maybe he hadn't seen her. She was unimportant. Invisible.

'Wow,' came a voice beside her. 'I saw it, but I still don't believe it.'

'I don't believe the mess they've left behind. Kelly, would you mind helping clear this up?'

'Better head back to work myself.' The first nurse sighed. 'Guess the excitement's over.'

Kelly tore her gaze away from the open door that had swallowed the figure of Tony Grimshaw.

Yes. The excitement was definitely over.

'Are you sure?'

'I've checked three times since you rang this morning, Mr Grimshaw. I'm sorry, but there's no C. Riley to be found on either the permanent or the casual nursing staff databases.'

'But…'

'Are you sure she's a nurse?' The woman from Personnel was beginning to sound impatient on the other end of the line. 'St Patrick's employs hundreds of people, you know. This Miss Riley you're trying to locate might be a physiotherapist or a dietician or a social worker—or any number of other things.'

'But she said…' Tony paused. She hadn't actually said she was a nurse, had she? She'd said she worked in a lot of different areas and that her favourite places were Emergency and Theatre. He was standing in the theatre suite right now, and there were people everywhere. Nurses, orderlies, technicians. Even a girl polishing the taps on the handbasins.

There were also two registrars waiting for him at a discreet distance from this wall phone. They were running late for a departmental meeting.

'Never mind.' He'd probably started some sort of a rumour by making these enquiries in the first place, but the staff in Personnel weren't to know *why* he was trying to locate the woman. It could be to reprimand her or something. 'Thank you for your help,' he added.

'A pleasure. If I hear anything that might be helpful I'll contact you, shall I?'

Tony could squash any embryonic rumours by saying it really didn't matter.

But it did, didn't it?

Since he'd woken up on Sunday morning to reach out and find his bed empty, he'd been unable to get rid of that sense of…loss.

It should have been easy. He'd thought he had it sorted when anger had kicked in briefly. When he'd started feeling as though he'd been used and discarded. But then the doubts had crept in. Excuses his brain was only too willing to come up with on her behalf.

Maybe she'd had a good reason to leave without saying anything. Mind you, there'd have to be a good reason to justify not wanting to repeat that experience. He knew it had been just as good for her as it had been for him. Nobody could fake that kind of responsiveness. Or sincerity. The princess had been genuine and he wanted to find her.

Maybe she was married?

If that was the case, fine. Tony wasn't about to break up anyone's marriage. It was this not knowing that was frustrating him. That and the peculiar dream-like quality the whole night had taken on.

But it had been real. Utterly different from anything he'd ever experienced before, but there was no denying it *had* happened. Or that the impression it had left made it impossible to forget. Perhaps what was really pushing his buttons was the need to *prove* it had been real. So that he would know what he needed to aim for in his personal life and never allow himself to settle for what had been on offer so far.

Mediocrity. Interest that always became infected with an urge to escape.

'Thank you,' Tony said finally, preparing to hang up the receiver. 'I'd appreciate that.'

His registrar had an armful of paperwork, and there would be a lot more by the end of the usual late Monday afternoon meeting where the cardiologists presented their cases. They would listen to histories, view footage of angiograms showing coronary arteries in various stages of blockage, grade people to score the urgency of intervention and draw up the Theatre list for bypass surgery for the next week.

There would be cases left over from last week who hadn't made it to Theatre because of emergency procedures taking precedence, and there would be debate over issues such as age and lifestyle and circumstances.

A tedious meeting in many ways. Tony was tempted to leave it to his registrar and attend to something more important. Like yet another check on this morning's trauma case. Seventeen-year-old Michael was in the intensive care unit, and he was still a sick lad but he was alive. Tony knew his save was the talk of the hospital, but what concerned him was whether the boy would make it through the next critical day or two. Whether he would recover without sequelae that could ruin his quality of life.

The two men he was leading into the meeting room now had been the other musketeers at the ball. Funny how it seemed such a long time ago already. As they sat down around the long table, Tony impulsively turned his head.

'Josh, you know a lot of the nurses around here, don't you?'

His registrar grinned. 'I'm working on it.'

'Ever come across a Cindy?'

The grin stretched. 'No. No Barbies, either.'

Tony's smile felt strained. This should feel like a joke but it didn't. He nodded at colleagues entering the room, noted that the audiovisual gear wasn't ready yet, and lowered his voice.

'Cindy Riley,' he told Josh. 'Tall. Long, black hair.'

'Not the woman you spent most of Saturday night dancing with? Blue dress with a lacey thing down the front?'

Tony gave a slow nod, hopefully not overdoing the effort to appear casual. It wasn't easy. The memory of that 'lacey thing' almost exploded in his head. The way her fingers had assisted him to undo it. The way her breasts had felt when he'd finally got to touch them…

'Won't be a moment,' one of the cardiologists called. 'We just need another extension cord.'

'She told you her name was Cindy Riley?'

'Yes.'

Josh exchanged a glance with the other registrar. 'And you're trying to find her?'

'Ah…yes.'

Josh grinned. 'Did it occur to you that she might not want to be found?' he ventured.

'What on earth makes you say that?'

Josh didn't respond immediately. Computer print-outs were being passed around, listing the cases up for discussion. Tony took his copy but ignored it. He frowned at Josh.

'It just seems a bit of a coincidence.' Josh shrugged.

'What does?'

'A Cindy Riley. At a ball.'

'Thanks for coming,' the head of the cardiology department said, then cleared his throat. 'We've got a lot to get through today, so let's get started. Case one. Sixty-eight-year-old man with angina occurring with minimal exertion. Investigations so far reveal reduced ventricular function estimated at thirty-eight percent. He has moderate mitral regurgitation. A blocked anterior descending, almost blocked posterior descending, and fifty percent occlusion on his left main.'

The screen flickered into life, and views of dye being injected into coronary arteries were shown from various angles.

Tony was having trouble concentrating. A combination of words had made a loop that went round and round in his head.

Cindy Riley. At a ball.

Again and again the name echoed and merged, and finally morphed into something else.

'Good grief!'

'Problem, Tony?'

His soft exclamation had unintentionally reached the presenting cardiologist.

'Not at all. Ah…could you just rerun that last shot of the left main?'

Josh caught his gaze for a second, the quirk of his lips revealing that he knew exactly why Tony had been surprised.

Cindy Riley.

Cinderella.

No wonder this felt so different. He'd stumbled into a fairytale!

He'd found a princess in disguise.

What would the modern-day equivalent of a dropped slipper be? A mobile phone, perhaps?

Dammit. The only clue he had to go on was that she'd been at the ball alone, and had therefore acquired a ticket by being a member of staff here at St Patrick's.

The woman from Personnel had been fazed by the sheer number of employees. She hadn't been up to the challenge.

Tony straightened in his chair, clearing his throat as he prepared to redirect his focus to where it was supposed to be right now.

For the moment he was satisfied.

He loved a challenge.

CHAPTER FOUR

'I'VE got a bone to pick with you, Kelly Adams!'

'Hey, it's my day off. I can't possibly have done anything wrong.'

'You could have told me.'

'I did tell you. It's Wednesday, remember? Flipper's appointment?'

'Not about that.' Elsie clicked her tongue, but she was peering behind Kelly. 'Where *is* Flipper?'

'Crèche. We've got a two-hour gap until the ultrasound. I asked Flipper if she wanted to come out to lunch with you and me or go and play with her friends, and the friends won, I'm afraid.'

Elsie sniffed. 'I'm far too busy to go anywhere for lunch anyway. I've got rosters to sort.'

'But I really want to take you out for lunch. A nice lunch. To say thank you for babysitting the other night.'

Elsie's sniff sounded even more offended this time. 'Yes,' she said. 'The other night...' She fished in her pocket and pulled out a folded piece of paper.

Kelly watched her open it, her jaw dropping as a slightly fuzzy image appeared.

'Where did you get *that*?'

'Tom was on the hospital website. He thought I might like to see some of the pictures taken at the ball. I got him to print this one off. We both thought you looked like you were having the time of your life, but neither of us could figure out who it is in that musketeer costume.'

Kelly couldn't take her eyes off the image. She was in Tony's arms, laughing up at him. He was bent over her, about to sweep her into a dip, probably, and every line of his body suggested a total focus on the woman in he was holding. It was such a tangible reminder of that night. Kelly could feel her heart rate picking up and a delicious melting sensation deep in her belly.

'Can I…have that?'

'Not unless you tell me who he is.'

Kelly grinned. 'I'll tell you if you let me take you out to lunch. Please, Elsie? I need to stop at the gift shop on the way back, because I've promised Flipper a surprise for being such a wee champion for her blood tests this morning. You can help me choose something she'd really like.'

Elsie refolded the picture and put it back in her pocket. 'I suppose I could escape for half an hour.'

'Let's get our skates on, then. I want to take you across the road to The Waiting Room.'

'You can't afford *their* outrageous prices!'

'Yes, I can. Just for a treat. Go on… Bacon and egg sandwiches. A real cappuccino…'

Elsie might be grumbling, but she was moving pretty quickly for someone in her sixties with more than a touch of arthritis.

The two women made unlikely-looking friends as they walked briskly through the main entrance of the hospital to get to the popular café on the edge of St Patrick's grounds, but there was a close bond between them. One that had been forged by a mutual love for the baby Kelly had been forced to take with her, way back, when she'd applied for the job at St Pat's.

There was a limit to how much Kelly intended to confess to the older woman now, however, which was just as well. Elsie was shocked at simply learning the name of the musketeer.

'Dr Grimshaw? The surgeon?'

Kelly cast an anxious glance around them, but other patrons, many of them in uniform or even scrubs, fortunately seemed intent on enjoying the great food and superb coffee.

'It was just a dance, Elsie.'

'*Was* it?'

Kelly pressed her lips together firmly.

Elsie ate the last bite of her sandwich in silence. Then she looked up. 'You going to see him again?'

Kelly forgot her resolve to stay quiet. 'Of *course* not!'

'What's so "of course not" about it?'

'It's ridiculous, that's why. We come from different planets. It would be like…oh, I don't know…a member of the royal family and a servant.'

Like…a fairytale.

'Imagine if he saw me emptying a bedpan or something?'

'Did you tell him what you do for a living?'

'Hardly. I didn't even tell him my real name. I said it was Cindy Riley.'

Elsie snorted after a moment's thought. 'Very clever.'

'Very temporary.'

'Your planets aren't really so different,' Elsie said as she pushed back her chair. 'You could very easily be standing on his one by now, you know. If it hadn't been for that dreadful accident.'

Kelly picked up her handbag. 'I can't regret any sacrifice I made,' she said quietly. 'Not when it gave me Flipper. She's my family, Elsie. She's all I have that's really mine.'

'I know, love.' Neither woman had risen to her feet yet. 'And I know that you probably don't even admit it to yourself, but there must be times when you're lonely?'

Kelly ignored the gentle query. She couldn't afford to go there. It was something else that would become far too real by talking about it. It would become real and then it would grow. She stood up.

'And that's another reason I won't be seeing him or anyone else again. I'm not going to risk letting someone into my life who might not be prepared to love Flipper the way I do.'

'You'll never know if you don't give someone a chance,' Elsie persisted as she followed Kelly. 'And who said you had to marry him, anyway? Or take him home, even?'

Kelly gasped in mock horror. 'Are you suggesting I engage in an affair that's never going to go any-where?'

'All I'm saying is maybe you shouldn't be throwing away something that's given you a sparkle I've never seen before.'

It was time to change the subject. Kelly veered towards the gift shop in the hospital foyer and the display stand of toys outside its door.

'Look! Wouldn't she love this pink bear in the tutu? Oh…what about this?' Kelly picked up a large, fluffy green frog. She hugged it, and then laughed as it croaked with a convincing 'rivet rivet' sound.

'Definitely the frog.'

The voice wasn't Elsie's. Kelly's head turned so swiftly she almost lost her balance.

Tony Grimshaw was dressed in scrubs with an un-buttoned white coat over the top. He looked fresh from a stint in Theatre, with his hair rumpled and a pink line across his forehead that must have been left by the edge of a cap. Dark eyes she remembered so well were staring at her intently, and she couldn't miss the sudden gleam of mischief in them.

'Still looking for a prince, Cinderella?' The query was deadpan. 'Try kissing the frog.'

Kelly heard a faint, "Oh, my!" from Elsie's direc-tion, but she couldn't turn her head because that would mean breaking eye contact with Tony.

And she couldn't do that because she was

watching the corners of his eyes crinkle, and she had to see the way the smile spread across his features. She could feel her own face changing. Mirroring his with a smile that seemed to be being pulled from a place she'd never explored. A very joyous place.

'What do you say, Cinderella? Can I buy you lunch and help you decide?'

'No.' Kelly shook her head hurriedly. 'I've had my lunch. But thank you.'

'You're not working today?' His gaze flicked over the civvies—a layered tops and the snug-fitting jeans Kelly had tucked into long boots. 'Or are you doing an afternoon shift?'

'No...I just came in to—' Kelly felt a nudge in the small of her back. Elsie might be pretending to re-arrange the display stand of toys but her elbow carried a very unsubtle message. It also provided inspiration. 'To look at my roster,' she finished.

'You'll have time for a coffee, at least?'

'Oooh.' Kelly would have to tell Elsie how sharp her elbows were. 'I guess a—a coffee wouldn't hurt.'

'And your friend?'

'Sorry?' Was he offering to take *Elsie* for coffee as well?

Tony patted the fluffy frog she was still clutching.

'Rivet-rivet,' the toy said obligingly.

Kelly had to fight the wild desire to giggle like a teenager. She also had to fight the acute awareness of the way his hand had brushed her fingers. This was like a scene from a comedy.

A romantic comedy?

'Here.' Tony took the frog from her hands and turned to Elsie, clearly mistaking her for the woman who ran the gift shop. 'Could you wrap this, please, and charge it to my account? I'm—'

'I know who you are,' Elsie said calmly. 'It will be no trouble at all, sir.'

'Excellent. Cinderella will be in to collect it later.'

'Cinderella?' Elsie managed to inject an amused but questioning note into her voice.

'Private joke,' Tony explained.

The statement gave Kelly a very odd kind of tingle. As though he considered them to be friends. More than friends, even.

'That'll be Miss—?' Tony raised an eyebrow at Kelly. 'It *is* Miss, I presume?'

Oh, Lord…was he asking if she was single? Standing there, in Theatre scrubs, looking just a little rumpled. Holding a fluffy toy with a look on his face that made her think that if they weren't standing in an astonishingly busy thoroughfare of a major hospital he would be kissing her senseless.

And now, thanks to Elsie, he was going to find out who she really was.

He *wanted* to find out.

'Yes,' Kelly managed. 'Miss Adams. Kelly Adams.'

'Excellent,' Tony said again. He gave the frog to Elsie. 'I'd really appreciate it if you could gift wrap this for Miss Adams.'

He led Kelly through the foyer and out of the main door on the same route she had taken with

Elsie not very long ago. 'I'm sure you've made a wise choice,' he said. 'You'll love the frog.'

That brought another smile to Kelly's face. 'It's not for me,' she said. 'I wanted to find a present for a small girl who was very brave this morning, getting some bloods taken.'

'Ah...a patient. How old is she?'

'Three. Nearly four.'

'You must be fond of her. What's her name?'

'Flipper.'

He gave her another one of those intent looks. 'Like the dolphin?'

Kelly laughed. What was it about talking to this man that had her smiling and laughing so easily? Feeling as if...as if that joyous place was just around the next corner.

'Her real name's Philippa,' she said, still smiling. 'She's always called herself Flipper, so now everyone else does.'

'You sound like you know her very well?'

'Yes.'

'One of the special ones?'

'Absolutely.'

Good grief, Tony was leading her into The Waiting Room. A staff member working behind the counter gave Kelly a surprised glance, which made her wonder how many others would notice her being there for the second time in less than an hour.

Tony sensed her hesitation. 'The coffee's so much better in here than it is in the staff café. We could go somewhere else, if you like, but there's not many places I could get away with wearing scrubs. I reckon there's more St Pat's staff in here than members of the general public.'

Yes. A quick glance around while Tony was choosing sandwiches and some fruit confirmed that. In fact wasn't that John Clifford—Flipper's doctor— with a group of other consultants on the far side of the café? Thank goodness he wasn't looking in her direction.

'There's a free table over there,' Kelly pointed out hurriedly as Tony picked up his tray.

'Perfect.'

It was. Tucked into a corner and at least partially screened by a potted palm tree. Tony might know her real name now, but Kelly could still pull a little magic around herself by keeping the rest of reality at bay.

Except that Tony seemed to have other ideas.

'So—tell me about young Flipper,' he invited. 'What's wrong with her?'

'She has…um….congenital heart problems.'

'Oh? What sort?'

It was so tempting to tell him something about her life from the safe perspective of seeming to be discussing someone else. Just to see what his reaction might be.

'It's complicated,' Kelly said cautiously. 'Patent ductus arteriosus with a major atrioventricular septal defect. Some valve abnormalities as well.'

'Poor kid.' Tony paused before taking another large bite of his ham and salad sandwich. 'She's had surgery, I suppose?'

'As a newborn.'

'Hard on the parents.'

'Very.'

'And she's been admitted again?"

'Oh, no!' The thought was horrifying.

'Why the blood tests, then? And the frog?'

'She needs regular check-ups. For all sorts of things.' Maybe it had been a mistake allowing this conversation to continue, but she had—so why stop now? 'She has Down's Syndrome,' Kelly finished matter-of-factly.

Tony couldn't know that his reaction might be under a closer scrutiny than might be expected, but his smile was very sympathetic.

'I take my hat off to parents like that,' he said. 'It's hard enough to cope with sick kids, but the ones with special needs on top of physical problems require an astonishing devotion. From everyone. Family, doctors, nursing staff…' He was smiling at Kelly now, including her in that number. Making her feel as though he understood and approved of any extra effort involved. 'She must be special to warrant a talking frog. What's her surname? I might know her.'

The belated arrival of their coffee was well timed. Kelly had a moment to stop kicking herself for talking about something so personal, however well disguised, and to look for an escape route before she could start clouding any dream with reality and making the mistake of believing it.

'You don't do paediatric surgery, do you?'

'It's an area of interest, but I haven't had the time or opportunity to do anything about it. I did have a seventeen-year-old patient the other day.' His smile had to be the most engaging Kelly had ever seen. 'Is that close enough?'

She dragged her gaze away from his mouth. 'How *is* Michael?'

That diverted him with startling success. 'How on earth do you know his name?'

'I was there,' Kelly confessed, delighted to have a new topic of conversation. 'I saw your thoracotomy.'

'I didn't see you.'

'I wasn't inside the lines. More like part of your audience. It was…amazing.'

'It was lucky, more like it. Good timing. A successful result is dependent on the level of cardiac activity, or on how much time between when it stops and a thoracotomy is performed. I'm not boring you here, am I?'

'Of course not.'

'There've been some big studies done, and I love to keep up with the kind of results of research that relate to what I do. Chances of survival are zero if the victim's arrested at the scene of the accident. Minimal—about four percent—if it happens en route in the ambulance. But you can expect a survival rate of about twenty percent if the arrest happens in the emergency department. Especially if it's isolated trauma to the thoracic cavity, as it was in this case.'

'So he's going to survive?'

'He's out of Intensive Care already. I'm planning to check up on him after lunch.' Tony stilled for a moment, as though struck by a new thought. 'Tell you what,' he said with a smile, 'meet me for dinner tonight and I'll give you an update.'

Kelly shook her head. 'I can't. Sorry.'

'Oh… Not a night shift, is it?'

She pulled a wry face which might easily have suggested the necessity and lack of enjoyment involved in having to work night shift, and Tony simply nodded.

'Not the easiest life, is it?'

'No.'

'But you've had a look at your roster today, yes? I've got mine right here.' A Blackberry emerged from the pocket of his white coat. 'Let's find a night we're both free.'

Kelly said nothing, aware of alarm bells sounding loudly. It was all very well for Elsie to recommend her putting some excitement in her life—and what could be more exciting than a date with the most eligible bachelor on the staff of St Pat's? In the city, even? But Elsie wasn't sitting here, realising just how easy it would be to lose sight of reality completely and make the mistake of falling for a man like this.

As if sex with Tony Grimshaw could *ever* be meaningless.

He glanced up from the electronic device, and must have seen something of what Kelly was thinking in her face because he frowned.

'I'm sorry I didn't see you in Emergency the other day. I hope you didn't think I was being deliberately rude?'

Kelly's breath came out in an amused huff. 'Hardly. Why on earth would you have been looking?'

'Well, maybe I was a little preoccupied at that precise time, but I *have* been looking—believe me.'

'Oh?' Words deserted Kelly.

Tony leaned closer. 'Do you have any idea what sort of idiot I felt like when I realised I'd been pestering the staff in Personnel to track down a Cindy Riley that I'd happened to meet at a ball?'

Kelly bit her lip. 'I never thought…'

'That I'd want to find you? And why not?' He lowered his voice. 'Why did you just leave like that, Kelly? Without even letting me know who you really were?'

'Because…' There had been a flash of something totally unexpected in his eyes. Something like bewilderment. Hurt, even? Did someone like her really have the power to dent the confidence of someone like Tony? He didn't deserve that. 'I didn't want to spoil the magic,' she whispered. 'The whole night had been like a fairytale.'

'Hmm.' The look was assessing now. Probing. She felt as if he could see right into her soul and gauge how honest she was being. But then he smiled. 'Fairytale, huh? I can buy that.'

He reached his hand across the table so that his fingertips touched hers. The tiniest connection in physical terms, but the effect was electrifying.

'It *was* magic, wasn't it?' he said softly. 'I was starting to think I'd dreamt it. Come out with me, Kelly. I'd really like more proof that it *was* real, because…'

The way his words trailed away made Kelly even more conscious of the touch of his skin against hers. It was spreading. Up her arms and into the rest of her body. Making her breasts tingle. Giving her that mind fogging curl deep in her belly.

'Because?' Her prompt came out embarrassingly like a croak.

'It was so different,' Tony said slowly. '*You're* different. I'm not sure why, but I'm a scientist and I can't just put it down to magic.' The smile flashed again. That disarmingly boyish grin. The kind that belonged to a man confident enough not to care about standing in a busy hospital thoroughfare in his scrubs, holding a ridiculous fluffy green toy. 'I think some research is called for here.' He moved his hand to pick up his Blackberry. 'How about Friday?'

'Flipper, have you still got the keys, hon?'

A small hand jangled the set of keys importantly. Three-year-old Philippa Adams was taking her responsibility seriously. She clambered up the steps to the front door of a small terraced house, and then stared at the keys, panting from the exertion of climbing.

'It's the big silver one,' Kelly prompted.

Short fingers fumbled, trying to insert the wrong key into the lock.

'Maybe I should do it this time, sweetheart.'

'No! Flipper do it.'

'I could just help,' Kelly said casually after another attempt, hopefully without making it obvious that this skill was still well above the little girl's abilities. 'It's been a busy day, hasn't it? I think we're both tired.'

'Mummy tired?' A round face appeared as Flipper peered up at Kelly. With its small nose and wide mouth and the almond shaped eyes that disappeared into slits when she grinned, she looked like an adorable pixie. One that was frowning in concern as she considered the possibility that her mother wasn't happy.

The keys were handed over. 'You go, Mummy.'

Kelly ruffled her sparse dark hair. 'Good girl. We'll both do it. You hold the key and I'll hold your hand on top. Like this.'

A moment later they were both walking down the short, narrow hallway of the tiny house. The two front rooms were the bedrooms, and a third door led to the bathroom. At the end of the hallway a single room ran the width of the dwelling—a kitchen-living area that gave an illusion of space, accentuated by French doors that opened onto a compact bricked courtyard.

Kelly peeled the anorak from the small girl, and as soon as she was free from her outdoor clothing Flipper made a series of kangaroo hops to reach the centre of a round rug in front of a small sofa. She held her arms wide and spun herself around in circles.

'Darn!' she called. 'Darn, Mummy!'

'I can't dance just now,' Kelly apologised. 'I need to make our dinner. Want to help?'

'No.' Flipper's bottom lip jutted.

'Hey! You dropped Frog.' Distraction was needed. 'What does Frog say?'

The smile erased the discontented frown instantly. 'Ribby-ribby!' Flipper shouted.

'And why did you get Frog?'

'I was a goo' girl.'

'You sure were.' Kelly stooped to gather Flipper for a quick hug, but Flipper wriggled free of the embrace. She swooped on the toy she had dropped in order to get her jacket taken off, and a moment later she was dancing again, with the fluffy frog clutched in her arms.

The bright green toy even had to sit on the table beside Flipper's plate when they had their dinner.

'No,' Kelly had to say firmly, more than once. 'Frog doesn't eat mashed potato. It goes in *your* mouth.'

As usual, it also went all over her face and through her hair. Flipper's bath was a necessity as well as a time they both enjoyed, but again the new family member created some friction.

'No. You can't have Frog in the bath. He'd get all wet and soggy and then he wouldn't be able to go to bed with you.' Kelly tugged on the toy that was being held with a grip of iron. 'How about we put him on the toilet seat and he can watch while I wash your hair?'

'OK.'

'And we'd better try not to splash too much tonight.'

Soaping the small body after the hair-washing was attended to, Kelly's hands traced the lumpy scar that ran down the front of Flipper's chest.

'We saw your heart today, didn't we? We saw it on the special TV, going lub-dub, lub-dub.'

'Lub-dub-*dub*!' Flipper's hands hit the water with enthusiasm, and Kelly laughed, wiping soapsuds off her own face.

'You should be called Flapper, not Flipper.'

'Dub-dub-*dub*!' And Flipper joined in the laughter with peals of the delicious gurgle that was Kelly's favourite sound in the world.

'He was a nice man who looked at your heart on the TV, wasn't he?'

Flipper reached for a plastic duck.

'I had coffee with another nice man today.' Kelly squeezed a sponge to let water rinse the suds from Flipper's back. 'He wants to go out with me.'

Flipper was pushing the duck beneath the surface of the water and then letting it go so that it bobbed up. Every time seemed to create the same level of surprise and elicited another gurgle of laughter. She didn't appear to be listening to Kelly.

'It's Aunty Elsie's fault,' Kelly murmured. 'She thinks I should go. She reckons I could hire another dress or wear one of hers. She's got all these wonderful retro frocks from the sixties and seventies she's never thrown out, and she wants me to go and try them on and she'll make them fit.'

Flipper threw the duck over the side of the bath.

'Do *you* think I should go?'

A ridiculous question to ask an uninterested child, but Kelly was simply thinking aloud here. Exploring what was, admittedly, a very tempting notion. Elsie thought she should go. She would be only too happy to babysit Flipper again.

'He wants to take me dancing,' Kelly told Flipper.

That got her interest.

'Darn!'

'Mmm.' Kelly touched the sponge to Flipper's nose. 'With the nice man. What do you think?'

'Man?'

'Mmm. A nice man.'

'Man darn?' Flipper was staring up at Kelly now, her eyes as wide as it was possible for them to get.

'Oh, yes,' Kelly smiled. 'The man can dance, all right.'

The stare continued, and then Flipper's face creased into that wonderful smile. Not that she understood what Kelly was really talking about. She was just happy because she thought her mother was happy.

Kelly lifted her from the tub, wrapped her in a fluffy towel and kissed her. 'I love you,' she said.

'Mummy darn,' Flipper said decisively.

Did she mean with her or with the 'nice man'? Could she make her own choice? Kelly kissed her again.

'You know what?' Her smile widened. 'I think I will.'

CHAPTER FIVE

THE exclusive harbourside restaurant was an intimate and discreet haven for those lucky enough to succeed in making a reservation.

It was a favourite haunt for Tony. Usually, the fact that the owner, Pierre, knew him so well and always had 'his' table ready for him was simply taken as a matter of course—by himself and by the sophisticated women who normally accompanied him.

Tonight was different.

It had been ever since he'd pulled up near the nondescript exterior of a terraced house in one of the less desirable inner city streets. One that he'd probably driven through many times with no interest in what lay alongside the road.

The surroundings had been forgotten, however, the moment the door at the top of the steps opened. Kelly had paused for a moment, scanning the limited parking spaces available for his vehicle.

Tony had also hesitated, his hand already on the door handle in preparation for getting out to open the

passenger side of his car. It wasn't because of any re-
luctance on his part, more from being struck by a
kind of wonder at the way this woman seemed to pull
light around her. Any background would have
become dull and insignificant.

She...shone.

Her hair was loose again, and desire kicked in as
Tony remembered burying his fingers in those luxu-
riant waves to draw her close enough to kiss. His
breath caught in his chest, allowing no more than a
soft, strangled groan as his body decided to relive the
exquisite tickle of her hair on his body when he had
pulled her on top of him.

Getting out of his car and getting himself on a
tight leash had been paramount. Tonight wasn't
about the overwhelming lust of the night of the ball.
It was about getting to know the reality behind the
fantasy. Kelly Adams, not Cinderella. This was a
date, and he was an expert in dates.

Except this was so different.

Kelly, with her hair long and loose, and a dress
that fitted close on the top but had a billowing skirt
with huge blue flowers splashed all over its white
background, couldn't have presented a more
dramatic contrast to his usual companions with their
neat, carefully streaked blonde hairstyles and slinky
cocktail dresses.

For the same reason, maybe, it was a little embarrassing to have Pierre greet him personally now, and
escort them to "his" table. He didn't want Kelly to
think that he came here so often. With so many other

women. He wanted her to think she was special. To know that *he* thought she was special.

A trio of musicians was tucked into a corner of the restaurant beside a small dance floor, but even that made Tony vaguely uncomfortable. It was way too soon to ask Kelly if she would like to dance. As much as his body craved the touch of holding her, he couldn't do it while things felt so...different.

Awkward.

Like the way her eyes widened when Pierre brought the customary French champagne to start their evening. He filled their crystal flutes and then stood back, a square of snowy linen draped over his arm, speaking in his perfect English with an accent that made most women sigh, detailing the gastronomic delights the menu had to offer tonight.

It would be easier when they were left alone, Tony decided. They could talk about the food and break the ice.

But Kelly's eyes were shining by the time Pierre had finished speaking. She didn't even open her menu.

'Pâté,' she said decisively. 'And the chicken with truffles. I've never tasted a truffle, and it sounded divine, didn't it?'

'Mmm.' Tony closed his own menu and returned her smile. He needed to find something else to talk about.

Something. Anything that would spark a conversation and give him a reason to watch her. The way those huge eyes took in everything around her, as though it was new and fascinating. The way her face moved to reveal so much of what she was thinking. She was so *alive*.

So real. Unsophisticated, perhaps. Childlike, even. Yet she was the most attractive woman Tony had ever met. And this was…astonishing.

Even more astonishing was the fact that the ice was broken by something that had always been a taboo on any date.

Him—talking about his work.

He wasn't sure how it happened exactly. He made some polite query about her day, and a responding comment about a lengthy meeting he'd been tied up with, and suddenly he was answering questions about his current research with an enthusiasm kindled by the interest he could see in her face.

'It's a drug that can preserve cerebral cellular function in patients undergoing bypass surgery.'

'Oh…' She almost clicked her fingers as she summoned the information she wanted. 'Like—what it's called?—Neuroshield?'

The surprise was a very pleasant jolt. 'That's the parent drug. When I was a registrar I worked in Christchurch under a surgeon, David James, who's married to a cardiologist. Amazing team. They collaborated in the first trials of Neuroshield and it's been in clinical use for years, but now there's a new generation and David wants me to provide an arm of the research project.'

'And you're keen?' Her smile advertised that she knew the question was redundant.

'Research is a dimension to medicine that keeps the fascination alive. The only way to keep us moving forward and improving what we're capable of doing.'

Kelly was nodding, giving every impression of being totally absorbed by the topic. Their entrees arrived, but for once the food didn't become a new focus.

'Neuroshield works by slowing the metabolism, doesn't it? Enough to preserve cellular function when it's being challenged by something like bypass?'

Tony could only nod, his mouth full.

'How do you measure the parameters of something like that?'

It was the kind of conversation he might expect to have with a bright house surgeon or registrar. The kind of junior doctor it was a pleasure to work with. Tony swallowed.

'You need extensive baseline data. Anatomical and functional assessment with a series of neurological tests including CT scans.'

'Sounds expensive.'

'Most research is. The major cost is paying the salaries of the people qualified to do it, but do you know what the real challenge is?'

She simply raised the dark eyebrows that framed those gorgeous blue eyes and it was all the encouragement Tony needed.

'It's finding people who are genuinely interested.'

'But why? I would have thought they'd be lining up to get on board.'

'It's not the most glamorous side of medicine. Not much kudos to be gained from the enormous amount of work it takes to run a project, collate and analyse the data, and then write it up and get the results published. Unless you make a major breakthrough, of course, and that doesn't usually happen unless you're prepared to devote years and years to it.'

'But you are?'

'I... Yes, of course.' Where had that hesitation come from? Inexplicable, but apparently significant. Enough for him to see a reflection of it in the way Kelly's eyebrows flickered into a tiny questioning frown.

'I've been heading towards this for years. Ever since David got me excited about the possibilities. It's a huge goal, but it's getting closer a lot faster than I'd anticipated. It all hinges on whether or not I get the head of department position.'

'I heard that was coming up.' Her glance was shy—as though she was so impressed she wasn't sure what to say. 'It's a big step up, isn't it?'

'Huge. And I know I'm young to be considered, but it's an opportunity I can't afford to pass up, Kelly. Imagine the influence I could have. I could make research a priority for the department. Attract funding. Employ the kind of people who will help it grow and succeed.'

She was watching him carefully, her food forgotten. 'But you'll miss being so involved in the clinical side of things? Theatre, for instance?'

Tony stared at her. He'd dismissed that as being a major issue in the interview he'd had with the board of directors earlier today. He'd believed himself. Who in their right mind would miss an overload of the pressure and tension that came with too many hours spent in an operating theatre? But could Kelly see something he might not have given enough thought to?

It was time to stop talking about this. If anyone had told him he could go on a date and have a thought-provoking conversation about his research and his career, he would have snorted incredulously. She couldn't possibly be as interested as she seemed. Or have any insight he didn't have himself. Tony pushed his plate aside.

'Enough shop talk, he decreed. 'It's time we had a dance.'

It was still there.

The fantasy.

The feel of a man's arms holding her and his body moving in perfect unison with hers as they gave their own interpretation to a superbly played medley of slow, romantic songs.

Not just any man, though. This was Tony.

Kelly glanced up, and another sense kicked in to add to her pleasure as her eyes drank in the angular lines of his face and the shadow of his jaw that the soft lighting accentuated. She could see the enviable length of his black eyelashes and she caught a whiff of rainforest from his aftershave. His formal white shirt was crisp beneath her fingers, and she could almost taste the kisses she knew would come later tonight. Every sense was heightened by movement.

Such intense pleasure. So much more than the first time they had danced together, because there was intimacy as an undercurrent now. They were playing with the physical fire they knew could be ignited between them. That they were in public again was intoxicating. Touching within proscribed limits, but the slide of his hand on the bare skin of her shoulders and arms sparking erotic images that had the memory of reality to inflame them.

His face was so close. She only needed to raise her face a little to be close enough to touch it with her lips and feel the roughness of that shadow. Touch it with her tongue, even, and taste the musky warmth that was uniquely his.

And then Tony looked down and caught her gaze. Held it for a long, long moment as he slowed their dance and drew her closer. So close she could feel his heart beating against her own. And then he smiled, still holding her gaze, and the moment was so perfect Kelly could feel herself being sucked into the fairytale.

The wedding bells.

The happy-ever-after.

Pure fantasy, of course. But what was the harm of indulging for the limited time they would be on the dance floor? The food for their main course would arrive at their table at any moment and they would have to return. To sit still and, to outward appearances at least, be in touch with reality.

But that held a new appeal for Kelly now. A kind of fantasy all of its own. She couldn't have the career in medicine she'd always dreamed of, but talking about it—wrapping herself in the edges of someone else's passion—was curiously satisfying. Intellectually stimulating. Balm to an area of her soul that had been closed off and left to wither.

Tony's ambition was palpable, but it came with an ethos that Kelly could understand and admire. He wasn't doing this for personal kudos or wealth. She had the impression that wealth meant very little, because it had always been part of his life. The desire to excel in his career was there because he cared about what he did for a living. He wanted to do his job to the best of his ability and he cared enough to want to keep raising the bar for the standard he delivered.

It was impressive.

He wasn't the golden boy she had assumed from a distance. A rich playboy who was in this profession for the status. If he was, he certainly wouldn't be planning to dedicate his career to research. Or to take on the demanding position of HOD and all the extra hours it would entail to further his dream. He certainly wouldn't be prepared to sacrifice the amount of time doing something he really loved—the hands-on battle to improve or save a life.

His research was fascinating.

He was fascinating.

Disappointingly, Tony was clearly determined not to talk shop any more this evening, having led Kelly back to their table. Wines were chosen and plates of gorgeously arranged and delicious food arrived. Kelly sipped her wine and then tasted her truffle-infused chicken, and she had to close her eyes for a moment to savour this new sensation.

She opened her eyes to find Tony watching her. Smiling.

'Nice?'

'Heaven.'

His nod was an agreement. 'I don't think I've ever had a bad meal here. You?'

'I've never been here before.'

'Really? But Pierre's has been an institution for decades now. Are you not a local girl?'

'Yes, but this isn't the kind of place my family could ever afford to go.' It was another facet of the fantasy. The snowy linen and sparkling silverware. Champagne and music and food to die for. 'And I...don't eat out much.'

His glance was curious, but they ate in silence for a minute. Then Tony reached for his wine glass.

'So where did you go to celebrate special occasions when you were growing up?'

'We had our celebrations at home. You couldn't beat Mum's roast lamb and her melt-in-your-mouth pavlova.'

'Mmm. Lucky you. I don't think I've ever seen my mother cook.'

Kelly blinked. 'Not even toast?'

'We had a housekeeper. Betty. She was a kind of second mother to us.'

'Us? You have siblings?' It was intriguing to

imagine Tony as a little boy. But a wistful desire to
see photographs seemed an odd thing to experience
on a first date.

And it was a first date, wasn't it? Even though
Tony knew things about her that no man had ever
learned before. You couldn't count the night of the
ball as a first date. Fate had thrown them together,
and for Kelly, at least, it hadn't felt as though she was
accepting an invitation to spend time with Tony.
More as if she was being carried away on a current
she had no chance of successfully resisting.

And coffee? Again, that meeting had been at the
hands of fate. This time, though, Tony had asked her
to be with him, and she had accepted—so, yes, this
had to be seen as their first date.

'I'm the baby,' Tony was telling her with a smile,
as her thoughts wandered. 'I've got an older brother
and a sister. You?'

'One sister,' Kelly said, hesitating only for a heartbeat. 'Four years older.'

'Your family still lives in town?'

'N-no.'

He got it, even before she'd finished uttering the
single word. His fork paused in mid-air and he
stilled. Waiting. There was a softening of his features
that felt like a safety net. He was a step ahead of
Kelly, but how on earth could he possibly know?

Could being honest destroy this fantasy? Make
the romantic setting and the wonderful food and the
prospect of dancing again insignificant? The reality
was harsh, but how could Kelly be less than honest

when he was looking at her like this? A look that felt like a touch of sympathy.

'There was an accident. Nearly four years ago.' She tried to sound matter-of-fact. 'A terrible car crash. My parents, my sister and her husband were all in the car.' A tiny quiver crept into her voice. 'There were no survivors.'

'Oh, my God,' Tony breathed. 'You lost your whole family?'

Kelly had to look away from the gentleness in his face. To press her lips together as she nodded. She felt her fingers grasped from across the table.

'Kelly, I'm *so* sorry.'

He was. The words rocked her with their sincerity. It was a gift of caring that she suddenly felt afraid to accept. She managed a nod, but then drew in a determined breath as she pulled her hand free and reached for her glass of iced water.

'Tell me about *your* family,' she said, changing the subject. 'I know who your father is, of course, but what about your brother? And sister?'

'My brother has a gift for languages. He's fluent in at least six, and did a PhD that explored similarities between some languages. Did you know that Japanese and Maori have some astonishing similarities? The same words for some things, even.'

'No.' Kelly was more than happy to be diverted. 'It sounds fascinating. What does he do now?'

'He started his career as an interpreter, and he's now living in Geneva and has an important position with the United Nations.'

'Wow. And your sister?'

'Meg did a PhD in physics. Of the nuclear variety. She lives in the States and works for NASA.'

Kelly's jaw dropped. 'Your sister's a rocket scientist?'

'Yeah. Pretty impressive, isn't it?'

'No more than what you and your brother do. Heavens, what a high-achieving family. You're all doctors! Your parents must be very proud of you all.'

'Satisfied might be a better word.'

'Oh?' Something in his tone made Kelly want to touch *his* hand. To offer sympathy.

'Failure was never an option in my family.' Tony was smiling, but there was a hint of something far less flippant in his eyes. 'My mother's a very successful lawyer with her own firm. Dad made millions with his construction company and then got bored. Local politics gave him a challenge, but I suspect he's looking for something new again now. His philosophy is that if you get a prize you don't stop. You just look around until you can spot a bigger prize.' Tony was turning his attention back to his cooling dinner. 'He's got a mayoral reception happening tonight, and I think he might be planning to announce a decision not to run for a third term in office.'

'A reception? What happens at those?'

Tony swallowed his mouthful. 'A lot of over-dressed people stand around, eating fancy bits of finger food and drinking a little too much wine. They seem very interested in everybody else, but what they're really doing is networking with people who might be useful in furthering their own interests. They're astonishingly boring affairs and I was delighted to have an excuse not to attend.'

Kelly's food went down her throat somewhat faster than she had intended. 'You were expected to be there?'

'My parents are quite used to the demands of my career. It's not often I *am* available to wave the family flag.'

'But…you *could* have been there tonight.'

'I chose to be with you.'

The look Tony gave her and the tone of his voice held so much promise. Too much. Any moment now and Kelly would actually start believing in this fantasy.

'I feel guilty.'

'For stealing me away from my filial civic duty?' Tony grinned. 'If it would ease your conscience, we could always skip dessert and drop in on the way home. It's not far from my apartment.'

He was planning to take her home to his apartment? A step further into his personal life?

This felt huge.

'I…um…'

'You might like to see firsthand what a mayoral reception is like. You could meet my parents.'

Kelly simply stared. Being invited to his home was huge in itself. Being introduced to his parents was even bigger. Reality was crowding in on the fantasy. Merging. Making those dreams on the dance floor a possibility instead of just indulgence.

This was dangerous. Exciting. Way too much to get her head around when this was moving so fast. Too fast. A romantic ride in a runaway train. One that was highly likely to crash. But there was no way off at this precise moment as far as Kelly could see.

She was caught by this man. He already had a hold on her body and her mind...and her heart.

There was no question about whether or not she could fall in love with him. She was in freefall. Was there something she could catch hold of to save herself? Did she really need or want to? This sensation was so compelling that for this moment in time it seemed worth the risk of whatever might break when the crash happened.

She could handle this. As long as Flipper wasn't involved, and it was only herself in danger of being hurt, then it didn't matter. Not in the big scheme of things.

The sensible part of Kelly was reminding her that she had responsibilities. That risk-taking should not be on the agenda. Her spirit was rebelling. Nothing ventured, nothing gained, it put forward. What if she took the safe option and spent the rest of her life wondering "what if"?

What if there was some magic out there and this *did* have a chance of working?

What if she stepped into his world and found there was a place for her?

What if he was feeling the same way about her as she was about him?

What if she said no and never saw him again?

Skipping dessert wasn't an issue. Kelly's appetite had fled and her mouth was too dry to swallow anything.

Her smile felt curiously shy. 'I'd love to,' she said.

CHAPTER SIX

IT WAS a palace.

Never mind that Kelly sat in a low-slung, luxury sports car instead of a converted pumpkin coach as she rode through ornate iron gates and up a long driveway lined with majestic trees. She was definitely back in the fairytale, and arriving at the modern-day equivalent of a palace.

Framed by manicured flood-lit gardens that featured two vast ponds with fountain centrepieces and blankets of flowering water lilies, was the biggest house Kelly had ever seen. The brickwork had been softened over time by ivy that crept up to the second storey, but there wasn't enough time to count all the windows before Tony eased his car into place with all the other sleek European vehicles accommodated in and around what must have once been a stable block.

There was enough time to do some counting as they walked towards the Georgian pillars that supported a roof designed to provide shelter whilst waiting for the massive front door to open, but Kelly was too distracted to think of it.

The lower floor of the enormous house was lit up like a Christmas tree, and heavy drapes on each side of the windows had been left tied up. Huge chandeliers hung from intricately moulded ceilings, and the light made the scenes within the frame of the windows as bright as movie clips for anyone approaching in the dark.

Someone was playing a grand piano, and Kelly could hear the muted background of classical favourites. A kind of steady foundation for the rise and fall of animated conversation and the occasional tinkle of feminine laughter.

Waiters carried silver trays of champagne flutes that caught shards of light from the chandeliers.

And there were people. So many people. Men looking glamorous in evening suits—a dark foil for the glitz of the women in their beautiful dresses.

Kelly had to fight the urge to turn and run. What on earth did she think she was doing? She didn't belong here. She would be spotted as an impostor the moment she walked through the door, and Tony would realise he'd made a terrible mistake.

He must have sensed her trepidation, because he caught her hand. But he didn't use the contact to encourage her to keep going forward. Instead, he paused, pulling Kelly close and then looking down at her without saying a word.

A second ticked past and then another. Kelly waited, holding her breath. Had he, too, realised that this wasn't a place she ought to be? Was he searching for a polite way to make an excuse and take her away?

Just the hint of a smile touched his lips, and he bent his head very slowly and deliberately to place a feather-light kiss on Kelly's lips.

'We won't stay long,' he murmured. 'I don't think I can wait much longer to take you home.'

It was the only encouragement Kelly needed. She belonged here because this was part of Tony's world and he wanted her by his side. That was enough.

Or was it?

Fifteen minutes was more than long enough for Kelly to change her mind completely. To have alarm bells ringing so loudly she was fighting embarrassment, disappointment, and something close to panic.

It started with the way people stared as she came into the first of the crowded reception rooms. Conversations trailed into silence, and Kelly could actually *feel* the touch of eyes running from her head to her feet. The men smiled at her, but the women exchanged glances and smiled at each other.

Knowing smiles that said: *Whoever the hell she is, she has no idea of fashion or style. What on earth does Tony Grimshaw think he's doing?*

Then there were the photographers. Why hadn't she expected that, when it was some kind of civil function and the local newspapers would be duty-bound to provide not only an account but plenty of fodder for the social pages? As a mystery woman accompanying the mayor's son, of course she would be the most interesting tidbit they had discovered so far. Lightbulbs flashed. Questions were asked.

'What's your name, love?'

'How long have you known Dr Grimshaw?'

'Is it serious between you two?'

Tony steered her through the reporters with the ease of someone who found being treated like a movie star commonplace.

'Take no notice,' he said to Kelly, even while flashing an easy smile in the direction of the cameras. 'And you don't have to tell them anything.'

He turned his head, must have interpreted her stunned expression correctly, squeezed her hand and grinned.

'Tell them your name's Cinderella,' he whispered.

That made her smile. It was enough to shut out the knowing looks and the flashes from the cameras. For just a moment it shut out the whole world around them. Here they were, the centre of attention because of who Tony was, and he was thinking of *her*. Making her feel as if she still belonged by his side by using a private joke.

Their joke.

The moment passed all too soon, however, and Kelly found herself being introduced to Tony's parents.

His father was wearing his mayoral robes, and had a heavy gold chain with a huge medallion around his neck. Bernard Grimshaw was as tall as his son but more solid, and had waves of iron-grey hair. The thought that Tony would look this good when he was in his sixties gave Kelly an odd tingle. Maybe it was the knowledge that she could spend decades with him and still find him attractive? It was more than good-looks. Bernard also had a presence that was a more mature version of Tony's charisma. One that made Kelly instinctively want to trust him.

No wonder he had done so well in politics. Kelly had her hand gripped, firmly but briefly, in a welcoming version of a handshake.

'Delighted to meet you, Kelly,' he said.

The sincerity might have been enough to chase away the horrible feeling of being a fish out of water—except all Kelly could think of as he gripped her hand was the astonished stare she was receiving from the woman who stood beside Bernard.

Tony's mother had to be the most sophisticated woman Kelly had ever seen in real life instead of in the pages of a glossy magazine. Blonde hair drawn back into an elegant chignon, with not a single hair escaping to mar its perfection. A black sheath of a dress that hid nothing of a slender body as perfect as the hairstyle.

In her billowing skirt, with its big, bright flowers, Kelly felt as if she had dressed in old curtains. Her long, loose hair felt about as appropriate as showing up to work totally naked.

'So you're a nurse,' Louise Grimshaw said after the introductions. 'How nice!'

Kelly got the distinct impression that she would have used exactly the same tone if Tony had told her that she was a cleaner. Or a fish factory worker. Or… or an employee of an escort agency.

She didn't belong here. With these people.

A waiter offered her champagne, but Kelly shook her head. The effects of any alcohol she'd had at the restaurant had worn off enough for her to realise that a clear head might be her only hope here. She needed to keep her wits about her if she was going to deflect the kind of verbal barbs Louise and her contemporaries could fire so expertly. A glass of champagne might undermine her control, and she would feel compelled to defend herself.

However sweetly she might be able to send the barbs flying back, it might embarrass Tony—and he didn't deserve that. He had brought her here in good faith. And he had promised they wouldn't stay long. Kelly could cope with whatever was coming her way. All she had to do was hang on until escape became possible.

Kelly was hating this.

Tony could sense her discomfort in the way she was holding herself. Taller. Straighter. Her smile was different because it didn't reach her eyes. Part of him was admiring the way she was dealing with something she didn't like. A bigger part was administering an inward kick for putting her in such a situation.

He should have known.

Any woman from his past would have been revelling in this experience. A chance to meet the movers and shakers in the city. A taste of being a celebrity, thanks to the attention of the press.

For some stupid reason he'd lost sight of how different Kelly was. Maybe that was because of the time they'd just spent together in the restaurant? The way it had felt to hold her in his arms again and dance with her. The spell had been reactivated. The one that made the rest of the world so distant and unreal. There had been a new dimension added, as well, finding out that Kelly had lost her whole family so tragically.

It explained so much. Like the strength he could sense in her. You had to be strong to survive something like that.

And no wonder she gave the impression of being independent. The need to stand alone had been cruelly forced upon her.

But she was an orphan and, no matter the outward appearance, she had to feel lonely. She needed comfort whether she was aware of the need or not.

Tony watched uneasily as his mother edged Kelly away from his side.

She needed protection.

His protection.

But his father had stepped between them now, and Kelly was being moved further away. Towards a group that seemed to be eagerly anticipating introductions.

'So…' Bernard eyed his son. 'Can I find you a drink?'

Tony shook his head. 'I've had my limit for tonight.'

Bernard nodded. 'Admirable restraint—but you're not on call, are you?'

'No, but I never have more than could wear off in an hour or two. You never know when there's going to be some kind of emergency.'

'Can't argue with that kind of devotion to your career, lad. Now, tell me about this Kelly…'

'Mmm?'

'Serious?'

Tony quirked an eyebrow. An effective 'neither confirm nor deny' gesture he had learned from his father.

Bernard grinned. 'Fair enough. None of my business. But—'

'But what?' Tony's words were quiet.

Both men turned by tacit agreement to look in the direction Louise had taken Kelly. She now stood on the far side of the enormous room, with a group that included a very pregnant young woman.

'She's…different,' Bernard said. His tone was a curious mix of appreciation and puzzlement. 'It's not just the dress. She's…'

'Yes,' Tony said. A corner of his mouth lifted and he was aware of something like pride warming him. 'She is.' He turned back to his father. 'So—are the rumours true? Are you planning to announce that you're not running for another term?'

Politics was a safe topic. A guaranteed distraction. Tony didn't want his father to talk about Kelly any more. To imply, however discreetly, that she didn't fit in here.

Bernard tapped the side of his nose and smiled. 'Wait and see, son. What's this I hear about *you*, more importantly? Sounds like you made a very good impression on the board of trustees this morning.'

'Who have you been talking to?'

'CEO of St Pat's. Have you forgotten that Colin Jamieson is a golf buddy of mine?'

'What did he have to say?'

'Said he thought you were a chip off the old block. That he'd never come across a young man so devoted to his career. Did you really tell them you have no intention of any family commitments distracting you from your professional goals?'

'I did.' And he'd said it sincerely. He'd believed it. So why did it strike a strangely discordant note to hear it said back to him now?

His father gave a single, satisfied nod. 'So it's not serious, then. I thought not.'

Tony opened his mouth. He was about to say something along the lines of being capable of choosing any goals he wished, and making sure he succeeded, and if that included having a family he would make it work—but he didn't get the opportunity.

A shriek came from the side of the room where Kelly was.

And then there was a contagious, horrified silence that spread rapidly outwards.

Tony turned to see Kelly standing beside the pregnant woman, her hand gripping the woman's arm. Supporting her?

Yes. The woman was leaning forward, looking on

the point of collapse. A man grabbed her other arm, an expression of deep concern on his face.

'Paige? Are you OK?'

'Good grief,' Bernard said. 'That's Nigel Finch— my deputy.'

People were stepping back. A woman lifted the hem of her long dress, gazing down in distress at an obvious stain on the cream carpet.

'Oh, my God, Paige! You're not going to have the baby *here*, are you?'

'No!' the pregnant woman wailed. 'I can't. It's not due for more than three weeks. Nigel! *Do* something!'

Tony was moving forward as others stepped back, but it was Kelly who took control.

'I can help,' she told Paige.

'Yes.' Louise was backing away quickly now. 'She's a nurse. She'll help.'

'Could you call an ambulance, please, Mrs Grimshaw? And you.' Kelly turned her attention to a couple beside her. 'Can you please get the table-cloths from over there? You could hold them up to make a screen and give Paige some privacy.' She was easing the woman to the floor. 'We need to see what's happening,' she told Paige. 'Are you OK with that?'

'Let Tony Grimshaw through,' someone called. 'He's a *doctor*.'

A cardiothoracic surgeon, Tony was tempted to remind these people. One who'd done a minimum amount of obstetric training, a very long time ago.

Screens were being held up in the form of long

white linen cloths that had been ripped off tables, scattering platters of canapés. The men holding them up had turned their backs. They opened the barrier to admit Tony.

Paige was sitting on the floor, peering forward as Kelly lifted her dress.

'Oh, my God! What's *that*?'

'The umbilical cord,' Kelly said calmly.

'Good grief.' The man kneeling beside Paige was as pale as the linen tablecloths. 'That's not supposed to come first, is it?'

'No. It's not ideal.'

Tony had to admire the calm in Kelly's voice. He might belong to a completely different specialty, but he knew damned well a prolapsed umbilical cord could be a medical emergency. And he knew what it took to stay calm in the face of an emergency. Confidence. Skill. A belief in yourself.

'We have to see how close you are to delivering the baby,' Kelly was telling Paige. 'What I need you to do is turn onto your knees, put your head down on your forearms and your bottom as high in the air as you can. Nigel, is it?' She looked towards the pale man gripping his wife's hand.

'Y-yes. I'm Paige's husband. The baby's—'

Kelly was helping Paige move.

'Why do I need to do this?' Paige was sobbing now. 'It hurts. I...I feel like pushing, and I can't do that if I'm upside down.'

'This takes the weight of the baby off the cord,' Kelly told her. 'I'm going to see whether the baby is coming and how far your cervix is dilated. If it's close, then I'm going to get you to push as hard as you can. Otherwise, you'll need to stay exactly like this until we can get you to the hospital.'

'*Nigel!*' Paige wailed.

'I'm here, honey. You'll be fine. This lady sounds like she knows what she's doing.'

She did indeed. Tony stripped off his jacket, flicked the studs from his cuffs and rolled his sleeves up. 'Can I help?'

'Don't suppose you've got some gloves in your pocket?'

'No, sorry.'

Tony's admiration for the way Kelly was handling this went up a notch. How often had they had personal safety drummed into them in their profession? Protection at all costs from the blood and other bodily fluids of a patient. And here Kelly was, kneeling in blood-stained amniotic fluid, oblivious to her dress being ruined, and about to give this woman an intimate physical examination.

It didn't take long.

'She's fully dilated,' Kelly reported seconds later. 'And the baby's head's engaged. Want to take over?'

'No. You're doing fine.' In the distance, Tony could hear the wail of approaching sirens. 'The cavalry's on its way.'

Just as well. With the cord emerging first, and the baby's head now engaged, its blood supply was cut off. They were only minutes away from tragedy.

'Right. We're going to lie you down again, Paige.

The safest thing for the baby is for it to be born as quickly as possible. Do you think you can push as hard as you can with the next contraction?'

'Y-yes.'

'Good girl.'

'You can do it, honey,' Nigel encouraged, but Tony could see the fear in his eyes. And the way he kept his gaze glued on Kelly as he gripped his wife's hand and waited for instructions.

'Pant for now,' Kelly told her. 'As soon as the next contraction starts, take an extra deep breath, hold it, and then push for all you're worth.'

Paige's knees were bent and Kelly was between them, her hands poised to assist a delivery that had to be fast if this baby was going to survive.

The siren got louder and then stopped. Tyres crunched in the gravel of the driveway just outside the windows. A door banged.

'They're in here,' someone was yelling in the foyer. 'Hurry!'

But Paige was pushing now.

'Keep it going,' Kelly urged. 'Harder! Push *harder*, Paige. Take another breath, grab hold of your knees and push again.'

'*Push*, honey!' Nigel's voice was strained. 'You can do this.'

Kelly's hands were hidden—presumably trying to get a grip on the baby's head and help it out quickly.

Tony heard an agonised groan from Paige, saw a rush of blood and more fluid, and then there was Kelly, holding the limp form of a tiny baby.

Paramedics appeared behind him with a stretcher laden with gear.

'Whoa!' one of them said. 'Looks like we've missed the party.'

'The cord's still pulsing,' Kelly informed them. 'But he's…' She stopped, focussed on the baby who was starting to move. Screwing up a bright red face.

The mouth opened and then shut. Tiny fists moved and the mouth opened again. This time a warbling cry emerged. The shocked and silent crowd around them gave a collective gasp and then an audible sigh of relief.

Paige burst into tears. So did Nigel.

Kelly handed the baby to the paramedics. The cord was clamped and cut, the baby wrapped in a soft towel and then handed to Paige.

'Let's get you to hospital,' they said.

'Hang on,' Kelly warned. 'The placenta's coming.'

Bernard Grimshaw was now close enough to see what was happening. Louise stood beside him. She stared in horrified fascination and then went very pale.

'What's *that*?' Her appalled whisper was loud enough for Tony and probably Kelly to hear.

'The placenta,' he told his mother. 'It's perfectly normal. You delivered one yourself three times.'

'I don't want to even *think* about that,' Louise said. 'Bernie?' Her whisper became urgent. 'Can the caterers cope with cleaning this up, do you think?'

'Shh. It can wait. It's a baby, Lou. Born in our lounge. How 'bout that?'

It was a baby, all right. A healthy-looking boy, now in the arms of his mother, who was being comfortably settled on the stretcher. A proud father reached for Kelly and gripped her hands.

'Thank you' was all he could manage, before emotion removed his power of speech.

One of the paramedics dropped a blanket around Kelly's shoulders. 'You're a bit damp,' he said. 'You'll get cold any minute. Just drop it back to the emergency department at St Pat's some time.'

Nigel turned back for another attempt at expressing his appreciation as he began to follow the stretcher.

'I... You... We're...' He gave up. 'Thank you.'

The thanks were well deserved. Would Tony have remembered the position a mother needed to be in to keep her baby safe in a case of prolapsed cord? Probably. Would he have been able to assist in a delivery fraught with potential disaster in such a calm and efficient manner?

Thank goodness he hadn't had to find out.

'You're a star,' he told Kelly. 'The heroine of the hour.'

'Hardly.' But she was glowing, and her eyes sparkled with unshed tears as she watched the stretcher disappear through the doors.

'You've had obstetric training, obviously.'

'A long time ago,' Kelly answered. 'And it was fairly limited.'

'It was enough.' Tony tucked the blanket more securely around her shoulders. 'You saved that baby.'

Kelly shook her head. She looked down at the front of her ruined dress and then scanned the room around them. It was only then that she seemed to remember where she was.

If she'd been noticed on her arrival, it was nothing to the attention she was getting now. Bulbs flashed again—and where on earth had that television camera crew materialised from?

'I have to get out of here,' Kelly whispered in horror.

'No problem.' Tony put his arm around her shoulders. 'My coach is waiting, Princess.'

Somebody started clapping as Kelly fled. Others followed suit. Then a cheer began, and the wave of sound could still be heard after the front door closed behind them. Kelly pulled the blanket more securely around herself as she climbed into Tony's car and fastened her seat belt.

'I really need a shower,' she said, as Tony started the car and headed down the driveway.

She sounded apologetic, but the mental picture of Kelly in a shower was anything but unappealing for Tony.

'That can be arranged,' he assured her.

'I'm sorry.'

'What on earth for?'

'I... Well, I need to go home and...'

For a moment they drove in silence. Tony didn't understand. Changing gear made something more than mechanical slip into place, however. He'd seen how modest the exterior of Kelly's house was. She'd just been exposed to the opulence of his parents' home. She was very wrong if she thought that a contrast in their circumstances would make any difference to him, but he had no desire to make her uncomfortable.

'I have a shower,' he said. 'It's great. Hot water and everything.'

The chuckle was encouraging.

'It's big enough for two,' he added.

She ducked her head as he sent a grin in her direction, but it was too dark to tell if his impression that she was blushing was correct.

'But… I don't have any clean clothes to put on.'

Now it was a mental picture of Kelly forced to remain naked for a length of time that was threatening to distract Tony from his driving. His words were a contented rumble.

'No problem.'

CHAPTER SEVEN

TONY'S apartment wasn't far from St Patrick's hospital. It was within the same inner city circle as Kelly's rented house, but it was a world away in every respect other than location.

The eighteenth-century, slate-roofed stone buildings had once been a boys' school, but had been converted in recent years to luxury apartments. One end of the complex included a turret, and Tony's spacious living space incorporated the upper portion of this turret as the main bedroom. It was the *en-suite* bathroom attached to this round room that Kelly was led into.

'Help yourself to towels and shampoo and anything else you need,' Tony invited. 'If you give me your dress, I'll rinse it out and put it in the dryer. If it's OK to do that?'

Kelly simply nodded. She hadn't uttered a word since entering Tony's apartment.

This was all so unreal.

Stunning.

The surroundings were a statement of wealth, but rather than being ostentatious they gave an impression that the man who lived here was dignified and intelligent.

Floor-to-ceiling bookshelves were full, but only the bottom shelves were stocked with medical tomes. Kelly could see at a glance that Tony read incredibly widely, and enjoyed novels as well as non-fiction. A beautiful antique globe caught her eye, and it took a moment to register that it was of the night sky and stars rather than the earth and its land masses. A powerful-looking telescope stood nearby, and a glance upwards revealed a purpose built skylight.

Gorgeous Persian rugs were scattered over a richly polished wooden floor dotted with leather couches. The deepset gothic arched windows looked as if they belonged in a church rather than someone's living quarters, but, while the room was quintessentially masculine and exquisitely decorated, it had the warmth of being a home and not just a living space.

A very special home.

The round, uncovered stone walls of the master bedroom were breathtaking, and the adjoining bathroom had somehow been designed to look as if it belonged, with its slipper bath and polished brass fittings.

What was even more stunning than the apartment, however, was the fact that she was here.

That Tony had brought her into his home.

Further into his life.

Still wordless, Kelly turned, holding up her hair

so that Tony could unfasten the zip on the back of her dress.

'Wouldn't want you to have to go home in a bathrobe later,' Tony said as he complied with the unspoken request.

Having undone the zip, he slipped the shoestring straps from her shoulders. The dress fell away, but Tony's hands lingered.

And then Kelly felt the brush of his lips on the bare skin where the straps had rested.

'Much later,' he murmured.

With a visible effort at self-control, Tony moved to turn on the shower. He picked up the dress.

'I'll be right back,' he promised.

Kelly was standing amongst the multiple jets in a shower that was almost the size of her entire bathroom by the time Tony returned. Her heart tripped and sped up as she saw him start to unbutton his shirt. He really did intend to share this enormous shower.

Would they make love in here? It would be a new experience for Kelly if they did, and it was just a little scary. Would it work? Could it possibly be as good as the first time they had been together?

Tony stepped into the steamy space. He picked up the soap and moved to stand behind Kelly as he lathered his hands. She could feel the whole length of his body behind her. His chest on her shoulder-blades. His thighs against the back of her legs. The hard length of his erection nestled against her buttocks.

Then his hands, slippery with soap, came around her shoulders and smoothed themselves over her breasts, bringing her nipples to life with sensation so sharp it was painfully delicious. His hands travelled to her belly, but didn't linger on their downward journey, and Kelly leaned back, tipping her head so the warm rain fell on her closed eyes and open lips.

No. This wasn't going to be as good as the first time.

It was going to be even better.

Wet.

Wild.

Incredibly arousing and intensely exciting.

And just when it seemed their time together couldn't get any better, Tony wrapped her in fluffy towels and scooped her up, carried her to his bed and made love to her all over again. This time so slowly and tenderly Kelly thought her heart might break as she lay in his arms, the beat of their hearts almost audible in the quiet moments that followed her final cry of ecstasy.

She must have slept then, at least for a little while, because awareness that Tony had moved and was watching her came slowly in the wake of a gentle touch that smoothed strands of tumbled hair from her forehead.

'You're amazing.' In the soft light of the moon through the arched windows it seemed that Tony's gaze was as tender as his touch had been. Then it shifted, to follow his hand as he slowly traced the outline of her body.

Down her cheek, over her jawbone and down her neck. Kelly could feel the pulse at the side of her throat meeting his fingertips. He followed her collarbone to her shoulder and then, so softly, shaped the curve of her breast. The movements paused as he reached her belly, his touch making a tiny circle around her belly button.

A flicker of new desire sprang to life and Kelly closed her eyes, waiting for his touch to go further. To where the desire would be fanned, yet again, into overwhelming heat.

But the circle was repeated. Slighter bigger this time.

'So flat,' Tony murmured. 'So perfect.'

'It just looks flat because you saw an eight months pregnant woman not very long ago.'

The pressure of his fingers changed. As if Tony was imagining what it would be like to be touching a pregnant woman this way. Kelly's breath caught in her throat. *She* could imagine it. Just the soft bulge of early pregnancy. Knowing that there was a new life growing within her belly.

A baby.

Tony's baby.

He would touch her just like this, wouldn't he? Soft, slow strokes. And when he spoke he would have that kind of wonder in his voice—the way he had just a minute ago when he'd told her she was amazing.

'What would it be like, do you think?' Tony asked quietly. 'To have a baby in there?'

He was thinking about the same thing. Did he also feel that poignant curl deep inside that could so easily become longing?

'If it was the baby of someone you loved, it would be the most magical thing ever,' Kelly responded.

Tony was silent for a moment. His hand flattened and became heavier.

'Do you want to have babies, Kelly?'

Another silence. Lulled by the feeling of safety that being in Tony's arms gave her and by the lingering intimacy of the lovemaking they had just shared, it would have been easy to ignore any alarm bells the loaded question might have set off. Caution came simply because Kelly feared she might jinx a dream by talking about it out loud.

'One day,' she said slowly, 'I would love to have my own baby. To be pregnant by someone who loves me the same way I love him. To make a family.'

Tony was silent longer this time. Long enough to make Kelly feel just a little uneasy.

But when he spoke his voice was sympathetic. Understanding. 'You miss your family—don't you, Princess?'

'Of course.'

'And you love children?'

The prickle of unease grew. 'You don't like children?'

'They're an alien species.' Tony was smiling. 'I've had as little as possible to do with them.'

'You don't have any nephews or nieces?'

'No. I don't think my brother or sister have even

considered the possibility. I guess families don't really go with high-flying careers.'

Tony had a high-flying career. Was he trying to tell her he never intended having children? Or a family? In the watch of her expressing the ultimate goal for her own life? A tiny shiver came from nowhere and rippled through Kelly's body.

'You're cold.' Tony reached out to pull the duvet over them both.

'You were lucky, you know,' he said a few moments later. 'You had a loving family and a happy childhood.'

'Yours wasn't happy?' Kelly had had that impression earlier tonight, during dinner, when he'd said that his parents were satisfied with rather than proud of their children's achievements. Asking such a personal question would have been unthinkable until now, but this had been a remarkable 'first date'. She felt closer to Tony than she had ever felt to any man before.

'It was privileged,' Tony replied thoughtfully. 'We wanted for nothing.'

'Except your parents' time?'

'We competed for their attention. Maybe that's why we've all been successful in our own fields? But…yes. Looking back, I think we all felt a certain lack. Maybe that's why none of us have had families of our own. Maybe we don't want to do that to another generation.'

'No pressure for any grandchildren from your parents, then?'

'Good grief, no!' Tony chuckled. 'My mother would have to start admitting her age if she became a grandma.'

Kelly made a sound that could be interpreted as sharing his amusement, but his words were a warning she couldn't ignore.

She'd seen his mother's horror at the mess of her carpet after the delivery of Paige's baby tonight. She'd been aware of the aura of perfection that Louise Grimshaw exuded from the first moment she'd met her.

To imagine her in the same room as Flipper, never mind accepting her, was a real source of humour. Kelly could just see Flipper whirling in circles as she 'danced'. Sending some priceless ornament flying to its doom. Her daughter had a lot to learn before her eating habits became less than messy, and she would take longer than most children to accomplish that skill. And, no matter how deeply Kelly loved her little girl, there was no getting away from the fact that, in the eyes of the world, Flipper was not 'perfect'.

It was a no-brainer. Kelly and her daughter would never fit into the kind of world Tony came from. It wasn't just his background. As a famous surgeon and head of a prestigious department, he would always have that kind of social life. And he didn't want a family anyway, so the writing couldn't be clearer on that mental wall.

This relationship was going nowhere.

But did that matter when Kelly had never felt

happier than she did at this moment, cradled in the arms of the most amazing man she'd ever met? It was too late not to fall in love with him. Why couldn't she just take it as it came and enjoy their time together for what it was, without ringing a death knell because it had no future?

'I'd be hopeless with a baby.' Tony's words broke into the whirl of Kelly's thoughts. 'Couldn't get away from Obstetrics fast enough, to tell you the truth. Messy business.'

'Worth it,' Kelly said softly. 'You must have felt that magic when Paige's baby started moving. Like it was coming to life in front of our eyes.'

'It *was*, thank God.' Tony's sigh was an echo of the relief they had both experienced at the time. 'I'm just glad you knew what you were doing.'

'But I didn't,' Kelly confessed. 'If anything had gone really wrong I would have been in deep trouble. I only did a short run in O&G.'

'Run?' Tony moved so that he was looking at Kelly's face. 'I'd only expect a medical student or junior doctor to use a term like that. Not a nurse.'

Kelly could see curiosity in his face. She could also see softness. And something else. An expectation that she could do more to impress him than she already had tonight?

Kelly wanted to impress him.

She also wanted to trust him. And he had just made it possible to take another step in that direction without compromising the safety of what was most important in her life.

'I *was* a med student,' she told him.

She could *feel* him absorbing what had to be startling information. Analysing the implications. Adjusting his opinion of her? He pulled her closer again, resting his chin on the top of her head.

'Somehow,' he said at last, 'that doesn't surprise me. You acted like a doctor tonight, Kelly. Calm and capable. How far did you get with your training?'

'To the end of my fourth year.'

'So you were ready to get right into the clinical side of things?'

'Yes.'

'You were doing well?' His tone suggested he expected nothing less.

'Top of my class.' Kelly's pride was something she hadn't felt for a very long time.

She could feel his nod. 'How long ago did you leave?'

'About three and a half years.'

'Did it have something to do with the accident that took your family?'

It was Kelly's turn to nod. 'It had everything to do with the accident. I...simply couldn't afford to continue.'

They were getting onto dangerous territory here. Kelly wasn't ready to tell him about Flipper. She could feel herself shrinking away from revealing that much, but at the same time she had to resist the pull to tell him everything.

To trust him with everything.

No. That way lay the potential for hurt that might

never go away. She could take it for herself, but she wasn't going to let Flipper be rejected by anyone. Not by Tony's mother or, worse, Tony himself.

With a bit of luck Tony would interpret her statement as meaning she had had financial problems. If he was as connected to her thoughts as he seemed to be he would also realise she didn't want to talk about it any more. It was a reasonable denial. Traumatic events were downbeat, and why would either of them want to spoil this time together?

If he respected her, he wouldn't push.

The silence grew.

Tony didn't want to break it. He lay there, holding Kelly in his arms. In his own bedroom but in a place he'd never been before. With this astonishing woman who made him feel...

Tony sighed, pressing his lips against her hair as he expelled the air slowly from his lungs. He didn't know *how* she made him feel.

He just knew that being with her changed things. That she was beautiful and clever. That she had a strength of character that blew him away. That she had so much to give and that right now he was lucky enough to be a recipient.

He wasn't going to embarrass her by asking questions about the financial difficulties she must have faced in the wake of losing her family that had enforced her dropping out of medical school.

Neither was he going to dwell on any aspects of their time together that undermined his intention of spending more time with this woman. In fact, when he thought about it, the way people had been cheering when they'd left his parents' house earlier could be seen as a stamp of approval. Of acceptance that pointed to the possibility of overcoming any antipathy to her being there that had come from both Kelly and the reception attendees.

So they came from very different backgrounds.

So what?

The things they had in common mattered a lot more. Like a shared passion for medicine. *That* was why he was able to talk about his work with Kelly and not feel he was breaking unspoken rules or, worse, boring her senseless. If her circumstances were different she might return to medical school, even, and join him as a colleague. An equal.

A love of dancing was something else they had in common. They were like two halves of a single unit on a dance floor. Lifted by music and so light they could fly.

And that was part of their physical connection that could be public. The private part was like nothing Tony had ever experienced before. Her response. Her generosity. Her…

What *was* the extraordinary sensation that came at the climax of making love with her? A feeling that they almost merged. That she became an extension of his own body. A part that he didn't want to live without.

A dangerous line of thought. Ridiculously fanciful. Totally unscientific and probably no more than hormones in overdrive.

Distraction was needed here.

Or possibly further research.

Tony's lips curved. He traced Kelly's face until he reached her chin, and then he lifted her face so he could kiss her lips. He wanted to touch her again. To taste her. To lose himself inside her.

With a groan of renewed desire, Tony drew back the duvet. There was no place for any kind of barrier right now. He felt Kelly's arms come around him and then the touch of the tip of her tongue invited him to deepen their kiss.

There was no hesitation in his response.

He was lost…again.

CHAPTER EIGHT

IF FLIPPER hadn't dropped her fluffy toy frog at precisely the point they had stepped through the automatic doors at a side entrance to St Pat's that led to the outpatient department, Kelly wouldn't have spotted it.

'*Ribby!*' Flipper wailed in distress. Still hanging onto Kelly's hand, she planted her feet and dropped her weight to act like an anchor. The manoeuvre was successful.

'What is it this time?' Kelly noted the downturned bottom lip with dismay. 'We're going to be late to see Dr Clifford at the rate we're going.'

'Ribby,' Flipper sniffled.

Kelly looked behind them and sighed. She let go of Flipper's hand and stepped back to swoop on the toy whose novelty had yet to wear off. The thought of getting through a doctor's appointment with the beloved object missing didn't bear thinking about.

Straightening, Kelly flicked her gaze over the big metal box that contained copies of the city's major daily newspaper, and suddenly any anxiety about the appointment or even reaching it in time faded into insignificance. Stunned, she handed the frog to Flipper and fished for the wallet in her handbag.

'Wait,' she instructed Flipper, a little more tersely than she had intended. 'I—have to buy a paper.'

It was difficult to feed coins into the slot that released a copy of the paper for purchase because her fingers were shaking.

Small bright eyes were watching. 'Flipper do it!'

'No, hon. Not this time.' But the coin slipped and rolled to the floor, and the frog was dropped again, on purpose this time, as Flipper pounced on the coin with delight. It was too hard for her to pick the coin up from the shiny linoleum, however. Kelly picked it up. She saw the hopeful look on Flipper's face and sighed again—but this time it came with a smile.

'OK—you do it.'

She stared at the visible portion of the front page of the paper as Flipper, her tongue poking out as she concentrated, did her utmost to slot the fifty cent piece into the box.

The photograph must have been taken without a flash. Otherwise she surely would have noticed a photographer getting that close. The moment captured had been just after Paige's baby had been born. Kelly was looking down, holding the baby in her hands, and it must have been just after she'd realised it was going to be fine, because even in profile her expression was clearly one of amazement. Relief. And joy.

'Yay!' Flipper had succeeded in her task and jumped up and down with pleasure as Kelly pulled the paper free.

The main picture on the front page was much larger. A smiling Nigel standing beside a hospital bed, his arm around Paige, who was resting back against the pillows, her newborn son cradled in her arms.

'Unexpected Delivery' was the banner headline.

'Baby Arrives to Reception for Mayor' read the print a size down.

Kelly took another glance at the second photograph on the front page. The one of *her*. A renewed wave of shock kept her feet rooted to the spot. The last time she had had a personal connection to a front-page story had been the dreadful photographs of the aftermath of the accident that had wiped out her whole family.

By a strange quirk of fate here she was again, but this time the article was about the joy of a new family being created instead of the tragedy of one being lost.

Kelly ignored the tug on her skirt, her eyes running swiftly over the lines of print.

Deputy Mayor Nigel Finch's firstborn son arrived during a reception held in honour of visiting dignitaries at the home of Mayor Bernard Grimshaw on Friday evening just after ten.

'Mummy?'

'In a sec, sweetie.' Kelly tried to read faster.

'It was totally unexpected,' Nigel was quoted as saying. 'And it happened so fast. No warning at all. I don't mind admitting I was alarmed, to say the least, but all's well that ends well.'

Kelly's gaze flicked back to the main photograph and its caption: 'William James Finch, weighing in at almost six pounds, safe in St Patrick's Maternity Unit after his dramatic entrance to the world.'

She tried to find the place she'd left in the article.

'I want to express my heartfelt gratitude,' Nigel said, 'to the nurse who assisted Paige. To the ambulance crew and to the staff here at St Patrick's Hospital. They are all a credit to our wonderful city.'

But she wasn't a nurse! Kelly bit her lip, taking another look at the photograph of herself. At its caption. 'Kelly Adams' it said in tiny print. 'A member of St Patrick's nursing staff'.

'*Mummy!*'

'Yes. Right.' Kelly folded the paper hurriedly, glancing around as if she half expected someone to point. To say she was the fraud she suddenly felt herself to be. Except she'd never *said* she was a nurse, had she? And an aide could be considered part of the nursing staff, surely? Papers were always getting things wrong.

Her picture was in profile and her head was bent, partly screened by her hair. Would anyone recognise her? Tony would know, of course, but that didn't matter because he didn't know what her actual position on the staff of St Patrick's was. It was those who did that could make this a problem. The people who could tell him before she found the right moment to correct his assumption that she was a qualified nurse.

If only she'd said something right at the start— but how could she have? And why? The reality of bedpans and mops was on another planet from the fairytale she'd stepped into at the ball. Irrelevant. And now he was so impressed that she'd been a top student at medical school. She'd been too proud to admit the spot at the lower end of the medical spectrum that she now occupied.

The sinking sensation in the pit of Kelly's stomach suggested that she knew the fall was coming. There was just a very slim hope that she could avoid the worst of it.

'Look.' She crouched beside Flipper for a moment, showing her the picture still visible on one of the folds. 'Who's that?'

Flipper looked. She beamed. 'Bubba!'

'It *is* a baby. A really tiny one. Who's holding the baby?'

Flipper squinted. 'Bubba,' she repeated, and then turned away, any interest forgotten.

Maybe it was premature, but the fact that Flipper hadn't recognised her own mother in the picture was a comfort.

St Patrick's employed hundreds and hundreds of people. Most of the staff Kelly worked alongside only knew her by her first name because that was the only name on her badge. Most would never have seen her with her hair loose. Thanks to the horrible shower cap, most would have no idea what colour her hair was, even.

Kelly Adams? She could imagine an exchange in a nurses' locker room. *You know her?*

Never heard of her. You?

No. Doesn't work on our ward.

And then it would be forgotten. By tomorrow it would be yesterday's news and nobody would care.

Kelly hurried into the outpatient department, pausing to stuff the newspaper into a rubbish bin. If she could put this aside, who else was really going to be bothered by it?

John Clifford, that was who.

'You're a bit of a star, Kelly' was the first thing he said when she took Flipper into the consulting room a few minutes later. 'Nice photo.'

'I…um…just happened to be there.'

'Oh?' The way his eyebrows rose made Kelly flush.

'I saw you last week,' John said with a smile. 'At The Waiting Room.'

With Tony. Kelly sat down a little heavily on the padded chair. 'Oh…'

The connection wouldn't have been hard to make. Why else could Kelly possibly have gained admittance to a mayoral reception? Everybody knew who Tony was. Who his father was.

Kelly was a nobody.

Was that why she could detect something like concern in Dr Clifford's expression? Disapproval, even?

That stung. John Clifford had been Flipper's doctor for years now. Both Kelly and Flipper thought he was wonderful. A father figure, almost, for Kelly. A source of wisdom. A rock in times of need. One of the few people who had shared the joy of the milestones Flipper was reaching. Someone who cared.

But he didn't think Kelly was good enough for Tony.

He couldn't see her in the role of partner to a renowned surgeon.

Or was it that he didn't see Flipper as being part of an acceptable ready-made family?

He couldn't be thinking anything that Kelly hadn't already thought herself, but somehow, coming from him, it was…embarrassing. Humiliating.

Kelly didn't know what to say.

Flipper, bless her, saved her from having to say anything at all.

She trotted towards Dr Clifford and held up her frog. 'Ribby, ribby,' she said, and then grinned.

Kelly watched the transformation of the cardiologist's expression. He feigned astonishment, and then crouched to put himself more on the level of the tiny girl. He returned her smile.

'What have you got there, young Philippa?'

Flipper hugged the frog and made it croak again. Her grin stretched from ear, to ear and was so happy Kelly could feel a squeeze on her own heart.

John Clifford grinned back. 'Goodness me,' he chuckled. 'Whatever next?'

Flipper gurgled with laughter and squeezed the frog again. The doctor ruffled her hair, a smile still on his face as he moved to sit at his desk. He took another glance at Flipper before reaching for the thick set of patient case notes. The warmth in that look was unmistakable. Flipper had touched his heart the way she did everybody who knew her.

It wasn't beyond the realms of possibility that Tony could be charmed in exactly the same way. If Kelly let him into her life—trusted him enough to meet Flipper—it *could* happen. Couldn't it?

Flipper came back to Kelly and stood beside the chair, leaning on her.

Dr Clifford was frowning as he flipped open the notes, as if he knew that what was in there was a matter of concern.

A trickle of apprehension ran the length of Kelly's spine.

'Why don't you show Frog to the other toys while I talk to Dr Clifford?' she suggested to Flipper, making an effort to keep her voice light. 'Remember what's in the box over there? I'll bet Barbie would like to meet Frog.'

Flipper obligingly moved to the corner of the room and upended the plastic container of toys. She sat down and pulled her frog onto her lap before reaching for a doll.

Kelly watched the doctor flip through the notes, presumably to find the results of last week's inves-

tigations. When he looked up, however, he seemed
to be thinking of something else. His stare was
curious and went on just a shade too long. Then he
cleared his throat.

'How *are* things for you at the moment, Kelly?'

It seemed an odd question.

'Fine,' she answered. 'We're doing really well.'

Oh, help. Would he interpret that as *Kelly* doing
really well by snagging the interest of someone like
Tony Grimshaw?

'Flipper's happy,' she added hurriedly. 'She
loves going to crèche and she fits in so well. She's
starting to learn her colours and her numbers, and
her vocabulary is increasing every day. I think
she'll be able to attend a normal school without
any problems.'

'And physically? You haven't noticed any changes
since her last check-up?'

He sounded as though he expected she would
have. Kelly frowned, searching for evidence of anything she might have forgotten to mention last week.

'We're very careful,' she answered. 'Our GP's
wonderful. She knows to get Flipper onto antibiotics
at the first hint of an infection. It's been over a year
since she was admitted with that pneumonia.'

Dr Clifford nodded. 'I'm thinking more of day-
to-day stuff,' he said. 'Is she active?'

Kelly smiled. 'It's hard to keep her sitting still for
long.'

'She still loves her music? The dancing?'

Flipper looked up. 'Darn!' She held the Barbie

doll by its head and bounced the legs on the floor. 'Dolly darn!'

Kelly's smile widened, but then faded. 'She does get a bit out of breath when she's dancing, and I noticed she was puffing when she got to the top of our steps last week. Elsie mentioned it, too.'

'Elsie?'

'My boss. She's a good friend. She babysits occasionally when I…go out.' Kelly dropped her gaze, catching her bottom lip between her teeth.

Elsie had babysat so she could go to the ball and stay out all night. And again so she could go out and end up at the Mayor's house, delivering a baby and getting her photograph on the front page of the paper.

But Dr Clifford seemed to have forgotten the publicity.

'The tests we ran last week have shown a significant deterioration in Philippa's condition,' he said gently. 'It looks as though more surgery will be likely rather than just possible.'

Kelly's indrawn breath was a gasp. 'No,' she whispered. 'Oh, please…*no*!'

Her gaze flew to her daughter, who had given up trying to make Barbie dance and now seemed to be getting her to try and kiss the frog. Intent on her task for the moment. Happy. She didn't need more surgery, surely? With its horrible risks and the pain and…

And she really ought to be listening more carefully to what Dr Clifford was saying.

Yes, she'd always been aware of the possible need

for further surgery as Flipper grew, but it had always been in the future. A cloud that had almost vanished over the horizon after so many weeks and months of doing so well.

The cardiologist was talking about test results that showed that the valves in Flipper's heart were not coping now that she was older and more active. That she was already in a degree of heart failure that was going to need management with medication, and that the possibility of complications was of grave concern.

'If she had another bout of pneumonia it could tip her over the edge,' Dr Clifford continued. 'It might put her into an episode of failure that we wouldn't be able to treat effectively.'

Was he saying that Flipper could *die*?

Oh, *God*!

'And surgery would be the answer?'

'It's the only way we can achieve anything like normal cardiac function for her. The procedure's a common one. There's every chance that the result would be what we'd hope for.'

'But she's *had* surgery.' With the degree of medical knowledge Kelly had acquired she knew it was a pathetic thing to say, but this was Kelly as a mother talking. A mother who wanted to spare her child the ordeal of open heart surgery.

'I know.' John Clifford's tone was sympathetic. 'I'm sorry, Kelly. I wish I had better news. I'm going to refer you back to the paediatric cardiac surgical team. Brian Grieves is the best in the field. I'll make sure you get an urgent consult.'

'It's *urgent*?' Kelly felt a wave of panic. She wanted to scoop Flipper into her arms and take her somewhere else. Somewhere she'd be safe. But she couldn't protect her from this, could she? She had to trust this doctor. And the surgeons.

She closed her eyes for a moment, fighting panic. This was *so* hard. But they'd been here before and they'd come though. She had to do whatever was necessary to look after Flipper.

'Kelly?'

She opened her eyes.

'Are you all right?'

She nodded. 'Is it OK for Flipper to go to crèche today? I'm supposed to be working after this appointment.'

Dr Clifford nodded. 'In the meantime there's no reason not to carry on as usual. We'll keep a closer eye on her, and I want you to bring her into hospital if you have any concerns. If she gets particularly out of breath, for instance.'

Kelly nodded again.

'I'd like to listen to her chest again now. We'll talk about the medication I want you to start after that.'

Kelly was running on autopilot as she helped undress Flipper. Smiling a lot because she didn't want to communicate any of her fear to her child. She even managed to laugh, along with Flipper, when Dr Clifford made a show of listening to Frog's chest before he put the disc of the stethoscope on Flipper's chest. She felt dangerously close to tears, seeing how large the stethoscope looked against the tiny ribs, unable to stop herself imagining them being spread apart to give a surgeon access to her heart.

There was a prescription to take as well, and an appointment card to see the surgeons. It was all overwhelming, and Kelly felt dazed. It was a huge relief to be able to leave, but John Clifford had something else he wanted to say. He walked to the door with Kelly.

'I know this is none of my business,' he said quietly, 'but I'm a family friend of the Grimshaws and I've known Tony for a very long time.'

Kelly stared at him. She couldn't think of anything other than what lay in the near future for Flipper right now. It was actually an effort to remember the beginning of this interview, when the photograph had been mentioned.

'You know he's in the running to become Head of Department for cardiothoracic surgery?"

Kelly said nothing.

'He has an astonishingly bright future ahead of him but he's very young to be considered for a position like this.'

Kelly continued to stare. What on earth could this possibly have to do with *her*?

Dr Clifford shook his head. 'Forget I said anything, Kelly. Most unprofessional of me. I…just think you have enough to cope with without…complications.'

It wasn't until Kelly had dropped Flipper at

crèche, changed into her uniform and gone to find where she was being sent for the day that she understood what John Clifford hadn't put into words.

Being associated with Kelly could undermine Tony's chances of getting the position he wanted. She was unsuitable. If Tony found out about Flipper he would end their relationship and she would be hurt, and she didn't need that on top of everything else she had to deal with at the moment.

Or maybe Tony wouldn't, but what if it made a difference to his success? He was passionate about his work. His research. What if he fell in love with her and it wasn't until later that he realised the damage it had done to his career?

Kelly had always known she had no basis other than dreams to imagine a future for this relationship. And didn't the magic of a fairytale depend on someone being given something they wanted more than anything else? Taking something away or even risking it was certainly not part of any happy ending. Now was the ideal time to call a halt. When she had far more important things to think about than her love life. John Clifford had hit the nail squarely on its head. She couldn't afford complications.

Flipper's heart was in more danger than her own.

Elsie thought she should take the day off. 'You can't work when you're so worried about the little one.'

'It's the best thing I *can* do,' Kelly said. 'Put me somewhere really busy, Elsie. Like Emergency. I have to work if I'm going to pay the bills, and if I'm busy I won't be able to worry so much.'

'They do need someone in Emergency. If you're sure?'

'I'm sure.'

'What's the blood pressure?' Tony was frowning, seconds after picking up the phone on the surgical ward's office desk.

'One-oh-five on sixty. And falling.'

'Jugular venous pressure?'

'Elevated.'

Damn. 'Have you ordered an echocardiogram?'

'Tech's on her way.'

'So am I. Check out the availability of a theatre, would you, please, Josh? We may need to take him back upstairs.'

So much for catching up with long overdue discharge summaries in his already late lunchbreak. The Dictaphone and patient notes were left strewn on the desk as Tony headed for the post-surgical intensive care unit.

He took the stairs rather than waiting for an elevator, but he still arrived after the requested diagnostic equipment, which was now set up beside the unconscious man, still on a ventilator after his extensive heart surgery that morning.

He watched the young technician as she angled the transducer, searching for any evidence that might confirm Tony's suspicion that this elderly patient was bleeding post-operatively around his heart.

'There!' she said. 'Collection of fluid in the peri-cardial sac. I'd estimate about fifteen mils.'

'Enough to compromise cardiac function.' Easy enough to remove, but if the bleeding continued his patient was in trouble.

'We'll do a pericardiocentesis, ' he told his regis-trar. 'If there's any evidence of further bleeding we'll have to head back to Theatre. You want to do this, Josh?'

'I've got ED paging me. Chest trauma.'

'You go, then.' Tony nodded. 'I'll deal with this.'

It was clearly going to be one of those days. Like yesterday had been. He wouldn't miss being on call for acutes when—*if*—he became HOD. He would find out some time this week whether his bid for the position had been successful, so it wasn't surprising it was in his thoughts a lot.

He put it aside easily enough as he started the pro-cedure to insert a needle into his patient's chest and remove the blood that was creating pressure and preventing it beating efficiently. The beeping of his pager was an irritating interruption.

'Can you answer that, for me, please?' he asked the nurse assisting him. 'Take a message.'

She returned just as he was removing the blood-filled syringe.

'That was Colin Jamieson's secretary,' the nurse informed him, a note of awe in her voice. 'He wants you to call him as soon as possible.'

Tony simply nodded, his gaze glued to the monitors which were showing an improvement in his patient's condition. Cardiac output was improving, and the blood pressure was creeping up towards normal limits.

The only reason he could think of why the CEO of St Pat's would be wanting to talk to him was about the HOD position. Maybe there was a new contract, waiting for him to sign?

The readings on the monitors steadied, remained that way for several minutes, but then slowly, inexorably, started dropping again.

'He's still bleeding,' Tony said grimly. 'We're going to have to open him up and find where it's coming from.'

His day had now gone from busy to impossible, but Tony knew they would all simply have to cope. As they always did. He left the ICU staff to organise the transfer of his patient and walked towards Theatre, unclipping his mobile phone from his belt as he moved. Getting some good news in the few minutes he had available right now might be just the lift his day needed.

The first words from Colin Jamieson were not quite what he was expecting, however. 'Have you seen today's paper?'

'No. Haven't had a chance to see anything yet.'

'There's a picture of Nigel Finch and his new baby on the front page. The baby that was born at your father's house on Friday night.'

'It was fairly dramatic.'

'I've got the press hounding Personnel right now. Trying to find this nurse that delivered the baby.

Apparently Nigel is keen to thank her, and get some more publicity at the same time.'

Colin Jamison sounded irritated.

'She deserves the thanks.' Tony kept the phone to his ear as he pushed open the fire stop doors to gain access to the stairway. 'She did a great job. But—' He went down several steps in silence, caught by an image of Kelly. The way she hadn't been able to escape fast enough after that drama. There was a modesty about her. She wouldn't like publicity. In fact, Tony was quite certain she would hate it.

The need to protect her was an irresistible urge.

'But what?' Colin Jamieson snapped.

'I doubt that she'd be keen to co-operate.'

'I spoke to your father about this. It was Bernie who told me this woman was at the house as a guest of *yours*.'

'That's correct.'

'Then perhaps you can tell me why Personnel has never heard of a Kelly Adams.'

Tony could sympathise with the CEO's obvious frustration. He knew what it was like to have Personnel unable to track someone down. But surely trying to find Kelly Adams would be a doddle compared to looking for a fantasy character by the name of Cindy Riley?

'I have no idea,' he told Colin Jamieson. 'Maybe the data base is inaccurate?'

'I intend to find that out, I can assure you. In the meantime, will you be seeing this woman again?'

Several responses sprang to the tip of Tony's tongue.

That's absolutely none of your business, wasn't quite the thing to say to Colin Jamieson.

As often as possible for as long as possible, didn't seem advisable either, given the assurance he'd made recently in front of this man that he was a single, dedicated professional who intended to stay that way, and therefore his young age was no deterrent to his taking on the demanding position of HOD.

'Not immediately,' he said cautiously. But only because he was on call today and tomorrow.

'Do you have a telephone number for her?'

'No. I don't.' His response was a little curt. Why *had* Kelly been reluctant to give him her number? He'd had to work quite hard to get her to agree to have lunch with him, and he had to wait until Wednesday for that. Was she playing hard to get? No. As confidently as he knew she would hate publicity, Tony knew that Kelly was not into game-playing.

'Ah…' There was a satisfied note in the sound. Much the same as there had been in his father's voice when he'd decided that Tony wasn't seriously interested in Kelly.

It rankled.

Tony made his own choices, dammit. If he wanted to get serious about Kelly Adams then that was exactly what he would do.

'I've got to go,' he told the CEO. 'I'm due in Theatre.'

'No problem.' The voice was happier now. In control. 'I'll deal with this. You can forget about her.'

Really?

Tony entered the locker room to find a fresh set of scrubs. Even if he never saw Kelly again, he was hardly likely to forget about her.

Not that he was intending to get serious about any woman, but the way she'd made him feel the other night... Holding her in his arms. Feeling she was a part of him that he wouldn't want to live without.

Funny how that feeling wouldn't quite go away. It was just there, all the time. A kind of awareness that didn't interfere with anything he needed to do but was very pleasant to tap into.

Comforting?

Tony snorted, pulling a clean tunic over his head. He was a high-flyer. His career was taking off and he enjoyed the thrill of riding a wave of success.

Comfort was the last thing he needed in his life.

Bumping open the doors that led to the scrub room, he pushed the awareness aside yet again. Right now, he needed to save a life.

CHAPTER NINE

IT WAS just as well nobody's life depended on how well Kelly could do *her* job that day.

Simple tasks like changing bedlinen and helping patients undress, or moving unobtrusively through a busy department fetching supplies or removing bedpans and vomit containers were about all Kelly was capable of managing right now.

For once it was a relief to be following orders and not having to think for herself. She could do this automatically and feel as if she had a tiny bit of control in a life that had just been derailed.

Again.

She'd worked so hard, and just when she was coping so well—when there was the new excitement of a possible future to dream about—fate had blindsided her and left her feeling helpless, in the control of forces she had no way of fighting. She had to go with the flow and try to cope with one thing at a time to the best of her ability.

Just as she had when the accident had happened.

When her dreams of becoming a doctor had been torn away from her and she'd found herself a single mother instead. She had coped then—somehow. And she had ended up with something so precious in her life that she couldn't imagine being without it now. Something precious under threat. That was all Kelly could think about. She hated being apart from Flipper, but it was another of those things she had no choice about.

Or did she? There was a mother sitting in the emergency department with her child near the bed Kelly was changing. The small boy had fallen off the couch at home and he was waiting for an X-ray to confirm a broken collarbone. He sat on his mother's knee, giving the that impression that he was used to having her with him all the time. They were playing 'I Spy'. Kelly envied the way they presented a solid unit to face the world.

Part of her mind at present was dealing with the necessity of being away from Flipper *more* in the short term. Picking up some extra shifts so that she could afford the time off when her little girl had surgery and a recovery period, whenever that might be. Her budget was too tight to cope with unforeseen events, and careful planning was needed.

'The lady in cubicle four needs a pan, Kelly,' a nurse said as she dashed past. 'And could you find a disposable nappy for the baby in two?'

'Sure.' Kelly finished stuffing the pillow on the bed she was making into its clean case and headed for the sluice room.

'Starts with "C",' the mother was saying to the small boy. 'Like "cat".'

'Car?'

'No. Good try, though, darling. Have another look. Over by the doors. It's something someone needs to walk with when they have a very sore leg.'

How wonderful would it be to spend so much time with her own child? To practise letter sounds or colours or numbers through games, accelerate her learning by having fun?

Kelly ducked into the sluice room and collected a bedpan, still warm from the steriliser. She slipped a paper cover over it and tucked it under one arm while she reached for a disposable nappy with her other hand. It was an instant reminder of caring for her own baby when the memory was in no way distant.

Had she made the wrong choices back then? To go back to work when Flipper was less than twelve months old and put her baby into a crèche?

Two medical students on an intensive emergency department run had paused just outside the sluice room door, and Kelly hesitated, not wanting to push her way between them laden with toilet necessities. And, as she often did, she eavesdropped shamelessly on their professional discussion.

'He had cardiac catheterisation four years ago, which showed mild aortic regurgitation. No symptoms until about three months ago, when he noticed blood in his urine.'

'Any investigations done?'

'Yes. He underwent cystoscopy as an outpatient and the results were normal.'

'Is he on any medication?'

'No.'

'How old is he?'

'Thirty-two. He's a vet.'

'So what's brought him into the department?'

'He's feeling very unwell. Pale and clammy, and has a fever of 38.6. Pulse is one ten and regular and BP is one forty on sixty.'

'Abdo?'

'Clear.'

'Heart sounds?'

'Diastolic murmur. Lung bases have widespread crepitations. Oh, yeah—he's got splinter haemorrhages under his fingernails as well. Quite marked.'

Kelly couldn't resist any longer. She stepped through the door and smiled at the students.

'Make sure he has some blood cultures taken,' she said. 'My guess is bacterial endocarditis.'

The students stared at Kelly, their jaws dropping.

'It's a classic combination,' she added. 'Infection, underlying valvular heart disease and splinter haemorrhages.'

She walked away, leaving the students still gaping, and for the first time since she'd left Dr Clifford's office that morning Kelly was smiling.

For just a moment she'd forgotten about her personal life and the forthcoming stress and misery. Just for a blink of time—but it had achieved even more than a lift to her spirits. It had reminded Kelly why there was no point in revisiting the latest worry her mind had chosen to gnaw at.

Kelly knew she had chosen the life that was best for both herself and Flipper when she had taken this job. Flipper was in a place where she had a peer group. Trained teachers who loved her and resources Kelly would never be able to provide if she was at home on some kind of social welfare benefit. The isolation of being a stay-at-home single mother would have been detrimental to Flipper's development and hard on Kelly as well. She knew she was a better mother through the stimulation she got from being with other adults, being at least on the periphery of the world of medicine she loved. It was a real pleasure to remember snatches of her training and to keep learning through observation.

And sometimes there were moments, like the one she'd just had with those students, where Kelly gained a deep sense of personal satisfaction from who she was and what she knew. Never mind that she had to go and deal with the more menial tasks that working with patients demanded.

Except that she couldn't get back into the department. A stretcher was blocking the doors, and a highly distressed patient was trying to climb off it, fighting with the paramedic who was trying to hold a bulky dressing onto his wrist.

'Call Security,' the paramedic called to his colleague.

'My hand!' the patient was yelling. 'Let go! You're hurting me.'

'Arterial bleed,' the paramedic warned the triage nurse who was approaching. 'Industrial accident. Partial amputation. It's been difficult to try and keep any pressure on.'

Kelly could see the evidence of that struggle. The paramedic's white shirt was heavily bloodstained. So was the sheet on the stretcher. So was—

'Look out!'

With a wild swing the patient rolled clear of his restraint moments before two burly security guards appeared. He ripped at the dressings on his arm but then stopped, staring in horror at his hand only loosely attached to his arm. The spurt of arterial blood fanned out across the floor. And then the accident victim crumpled into a heap as he fainted. The paramedics grabbed dressings and applied pressure to the wound, and the security guards hovered.

'Get him into Resus One,' the triage nurse directed. 'I'll call the trauma team.' She took a look over her shoulder at the astonishing area the blood had managed to cover. 'Kelly—clean this up, please? As fast as you can.'

This was more urgent than bedpans or nappies. Kelly raced back to the sluice room and donned a heavy plastic apron. She made sure her hair was completely tucked under her cap and donned some bright green rubber gloves as her stainless steel bucket was filling with near boiling water. She took a large bottle of the bleach-based disinfectant needed to deal with a spill of potentially infectious body fluids, and also an armful of small bright orange plastic cones which would demarcate the area and keep people clear. She'd have to come back for the "Caution Wet Floor" sign.

Armed with all her gear, Kelly set to work. She mopped, rinsed the mop, squeezed it through the roller mechanism on top of the bucket, squirted liberal doses of disinfectant around and mopped again. The urgency of the task was helpful, because it stopped her thoughts reverting to her worry about Flipper, so she concentrated hard on finding every drop of blood and eradicating its threat.

'Kelly? Kelly Adams?'

The voice was loud enough to be startling. About to insert the mop into the steaming bucket once more, Kelly froze, turned and looked up.

A flash went off.

'What the—?' Kelly stared at the photographer. 'What the hell do you think you're *doing*?'

'You *are* Kelly Adams?'

Why was this man taking her picture? Why now, when she looked…? Oh, God! Kelly was clutching a mop, wearing an oversized apron, rubber gloves and her shower cap hat.

'You're a cleaner?' the man queried.

'No, she's a nurse aide.' Another staff member was approaching. 'Who are you and what are you doing in here?'

'I'm covering a story about St Pat's ED and its staff. Didn't anyone tell you?'

'No,' the nurse said coldly. 'Where's your security clearance?'

'Damn…must have forgotten it.' The stranger didn't sound overly concerned, however. He was checking the image he had scored on his digital camera. 'Great photo. Wanna see it, Kelly?'

'No.'

'Get out,' the nurse commanded. 'If you're not out of here in thirty seconds I'm calling Security.' She looked away from the photographer's rapidly retreating figure to raise her eyebrows at Kelly. 'What was *that* about?'

Kelly tried to damp down a nameless fear. She shook her head. 'I have no idea.'

'Neither do I, but let's hope that's the end of it. Let me know if he comes back.'

The photographer didn't come back. Kelly was left alone to get through what seemed an interminable shift when all she wanted was to get home with Flipper. To spend her evening with cuddles and stories and music and dancing and forget about the day.

Oh, God! Was it still safe to let Flipper dance? How could she know how well her heart might be coping with the stress of activity like that? What would happen if it wasn't? Kelly wished she hadn't been so dazed at the end of that appointment with Dr Clifford. She had so many questions she wanted to ask now. Would Flipper simply become more breathless with any exacerbation of her heart failure? Could she faint? Have a cardiac arrest and need CPR? The fear was going to be crippling, wasn't it?

'Kelly?' The nurse who had dealt with the photographer earlier that afternoon was staring at her with such a strange expression Kelly wondered if she had been talking out loud to herself.

'Mmm?'

'I've just had the weirdest call. From Colin Jamieson's secretary.'

'Who's Colin Jamieson?'

'The CEO of St Pat's. He wants to see you. In his office.'

'What?' Kelly blinked. 'What on earth for?'

'She didn't say. She just said it was urgent.'

Kelly could feel the blood draining from her face. Something had happened to Flipper. Something terrible. If the CEO was involved it must be bad enough for it to have potential consequences for St Patrick's.

'Are you all right, Kelly?'

'Just tell me…where do I find his office?'

Tony rapped on the door.

'Enter.'

It wasn't the first time he'd gone into the luxurious top-floor office suite that belonged to St Pat's CEO, and he wasn't about to waste time enjoying the view or the décor.

'Ah…Tony. Glad you could make it.'

'It sounded urgent. I haven't got much time, though. I'm sorry, Colin. I'm a bit tied up in ICU with a post-op case.'

'I shouldn't need to keep you long. Come in— don't stand by the door.'

Tony took a step or two into the office, feeling somewhat out of place in here wearing his scrubs. Two wing-backed leather chairs were positioned in front of the massive mahogany desk that Colin Jamieson was ensconced behind, and it wasn't until Tony had moved forward that he realised one of the chairs was occupied.

'*Kelly*! What on earth are you doing in here?'

She looked dreadful. As white as a sheet. Her hair was bundled into a theatre-style cap, but she wasn't wearing scrubs as he was. She had a smock on like the cleaners wore and… Good grief—was that a pair of rubber gloves she had clutched in one hand?

'Take a look at this,' Colin Jamieson commanded. He tapped a sheet of paper on the desk in front of him. 'The editor-in-chief of the *Chronicle* gave me the courtesy of advance warning on the article that's been written to accompany this picture.'

It was a picture of Kelly. Looking startled. Holding a mop and standing beside a bucket. Wearing the kind of gloves she now had in her hands. Looking, for all the world, like a…*hospital cleaner*?

'I don't understand,' Tony said.

'No,' Colin snapped. 'I don't suppose you would, having told me today that you had no idea why Miss Adams' name couldn't be found on the database of nursing staff at St Patrick's.'

Tony was staring at Kelly. She met his gaze, but only for a heartbeat. She looked terrified. Of *him*?

'Miss Adams is a member of the domestic staff here,' the CEO informed him. 'She is a nurse aide.

A casual staff member. It was quite a task to track her down.'

Tony was trying to catch Kelly's gaze again. What on earth was going on here? Whatever it was, she didn't have to be so frightened, surely? He didn't believe she had done anything so terribly wrong.

'Just how long have you been masquerading as a qualified nurse, Miss Adams?'

Her chin lifted. Her voice sounded a lot stronger than Tony might have expected. 'I...I haven't.'

'Dr Grimshaw believed you were a nurse.'

'I never *said* I was a nurse.'

She hadn't, had she? 'I met Kelly at the hospital ball,' Tony told Colin Jamieson. 'I knew she was on the staff. I made an assumption about her level of qualification.'

'Which wasn't corrected?'

'I...no, I suppose not. We haven't spent much time together since then.'

And the time they *had* spent together they'd had far more important things to talk about. Like his work. His research. His family. Good grief, how much did he really know about this woman?

'You've spent enough time together for you to have taken her to your father's house as your... companion.'

Tony frowned. He didn't like whatever implication the CEO was making with that tone.

'Enough time to allow her to fraudulently practise medicine in public.'

'Excuse me?' Tony looked from Kelly back to Colin. 'What on *earth* are you talking about?'

'Obstetrics,' Colin snapped. 'Delivering a baby. One presenting with complications that could have been serious, according to the specialists I've spoken with today. The specialists that some journalist from the *Chronicle* has also been having a conversation with, I might add.'

'Kelly knew what she doing. She dealt competently with a situation that occurred well away from any hospital. She was administering first aid.'

'From what I've discovered, Miss Adams does not even hold a certificate in first aid. She has no medical qualifications whatsoever!'

'She attended medical school,' Tony snapped back. The shock of seeing Kelly dressed in a uniform that marked her as being on the lower ranks of hospital employment was wearing off. He could understand why she hadn't told him because, to his own consternation, he knew it might have influenced his decision to keep seeing her. Now he knew her well enough to know it didn't matter. 'Her marks were excellent. Isn't that right, Kelly?'

She was avoiding his gaze again. 'Yes.'

'You dropped out of medical school, didn't you, Miss Adams?'

The response was quieter this time. 'Yes.'

'So as far as the general public is concerned this baby was delivered by someone who had no right to be involved. Our city's deputy mayor is horrified. So is your father, I might add, Tony. If this actually hits the papers, St Patrick's is going to have one hell of a lot of damage control to do.'

Tony eyed the picture on his desk. '*If* it hits the papers?'

'The editor-in-chief happens to owe me a favour. I've managed to put a lid on the story for the moment. If I can deal with it to the satisfaction of all the public figures involved, it's possible we can bury this whole sorry mess. And I *am* dealing with it. Miss Adams—your employment, casual or otherwise, with St Patrick's is herewith terminated. Please collect your belongings, hand in your uniform and anything else you have which is hospital property, and be off the premises within thirty minutes.'

'Hang on!' Tony was as shocked as he knew Kelly must be. 'You can't do that.'

'It's all right, Tony.' Kelly was standing up. The stained smock, the horrible hat, even those ridiculous rubber gloves seemed to fade into the background. The fierce glow of a dignity that it must have required enormous strength to summon made her physical appearance irrelevant. 'Mr Jamieson is simply doing what he has to do. I have no intention of making trouble for St Patrick's, and I apologise for the inconvenience I've already caused.'

She cast a fleeting look at Tony as she left the room. One that conveyed a misery that gave him a stab of discomfort in his gut. It was full of apology as well. To him.

He tried to send a silent message back. One that said this would be all right. That it was *his* fault she was in trouble and that he would do something about it.

The way Kelly continued smoothly to the door

and then let herself out of the office made him feel he had failed.

He got to his feet, intending to follow her, but the clipped voice of the CEO made him pause.

'I wouldn't do that if I were you, Tony,' Colin Jamieson said coolly. 'The way I see it, this sorry business has now been dealt with.'

'I'm not so sure about that.'

'Well, be sure about this.' Colin reached for the printout of the photograph and tapped it. 'If you continue your association with Miss Adams, you can kiss goodbye to any aspirations you have to head the cardiothoracic surgical department here at St Patrick's.'

CHAPTER TEN

HER life hadn't simply been derailed.

It was travelling at alarming speed into a chasm that appeared terrifyingly bottomless.

Kelly had to push the buttons for the elevator more than once because her tears were blinding her. It took an agonisingly long time for the elevator to arrive and for the doors to open, and just when those doors were closing again and she thought she was safe a hand broke the beam and made them open again.

Tony Grimshaw stepped into the small space.

'Hey!' He was peering at her with deep concern written on his features as the doors slid closed behind him. 'Are you OK?'

A strange sound halfway between a strangled sob and laughter escaped Kelly's throat.

Tony groaned. 'Stupid question! Come here.'

He pulled her into his arms. He tugged off her cap and took the gloves from her hand and threw them into the corner of the elevator. And then he wrapped her even more closely against the solid wall of his chest.

Had he pushed the button for the ground floor? Unlike her desperate wait for the elevator to arrive, it would be no time at all before it descended. Precious seconds to feel the comfort of Tony's arms holding her.

'It'll be all right,' Tony was saying, his lips against her hair. 'You'll see. I'll talk to my father. To Nigel Finch. I'll sort this out and make sure you get your job back.'

'No.' Kelly shook her head. 'You can't.'

'Of course I can. I *want* to. This is my fault, Kelly. I took you to that reception. I stood back and let you deliver that baby. This is crazy.' She could hear an edge of anger in his voice now. 'Just because you haven't got a piece of paper to say you're qualified it doesn't mean you didn't save that baby's life.'

'No.' With a huge effort Kelly pushed away from the wonderful warmth and solidity of Tony's chest. The doors of the elevator slid open and she stepped back, breaking all physical contact.

Feeling as if her heart was breaking at the same time, Kelly took a deep breath. 'You can't involve yourself with this, Tony.'

'Why the hell not?'

'Because it will cause more trouble. You…' Kelly dragged in another breath. She had to find out if there was any truth in that unspoken warning John Clifford had been trying to give her. Lord, was it only this morning? 'It would mean you didn't get the job as HOD.'

Tony's eyes narrowed. 'What did Jamieson say to you?' His huff of breath was incredulous. 'Never mind. I can guess. Don't let him intimidate you, Kelly. I'm certainly not going to. He's not the only voice on that board of trustees.'

So it *was* true. But Tony was prepared to risk a job he wanted very badly for her sake.

God, she loved this man. Heart and soul.

Too much to let him risk ruining his career for her sake. He was angry himself, now. Outraged. He needed time to think about this. To realise how much damage defending her might bring.

A chance to decide if being with her was worth the fallout.

And if he did? What would that give them? An opportunity to continue a passionate affair that was going nowhere? Tony didn't see a family in his future, and family was the driving force of Kelly's life—wasn't it?

Family.

Flipper.

Kelly had no more choice here than she'd had years ago, when she had chosen to forsake her own career. From now on she had to focus on the most important person in her life. The vulnerable one who had only her to depend on.

Her daughter.

'It's over, Tony,' she heard herself saying in a strangely tight voice that didn't sound anything like herself. 'We can't see each other again. There's no point.' She glanced over her shoulder to check that no one in the foyer was listening to this exchange. 'There never was.'

The flicker of shock in his eyes sent a shaft of pain through Kelly.

'Because of this mess? I can sort it out. I promise.'

'I don't want you to.' Kelly stood up straighter. 'I can look after myself. I…I don't need you, Tony.'

'And you don't want me, either? Is that what you're saying?' Shock had given way to disbelief.

Was he thinking of their intimate moments together and wondering how anything in their right mind could *not* want that?

Flipper.

The name echoed in Kelly's mind. This had to be about Flipper. Forget about herself. Forget about Tony. Forget any of those dreams of what might have been.

This was agony, but it had to be done.

'Yes,' Kelly said, her tone wooden. 'That's exactly what I'm saying.'

'Oh, my dear! You look terrible!'

'Gee, thanks, Elsie.' Kelly's smile was wry. If her looks reflected the state her life was in right now, she must look a fright indeed. She had a sick child, no current means of supporting herself and that child, and she had just pushed the man she would probably love more than any other in her lifetime firmly out of her life. With a sigh, Kelly pulled her front door open wider. 'Come on in, Elsie.'

'I don't want to interrupt your day, dear.'

Kelly's laugh sounded hollow. 'Are you kidding?

We've almost run out of things to do and it's only lunchtime.' She found a more convincing smile for her former boss. 'Please come in. Flipper will be delighted to see your face. Would you like a cup of tea?'

'I'd love one.' Elsie followed her down the hallway.

'Don't trip on these toys,' Kelly warned. 'The place is a bit of a mess. I'm sorry.'

More toys and a big-piece jigsaw puzzle of a clown that was half finished lay on the rug in the living area. Flipper was also lying on the rug, chewing on the lower legs of the clown. Her own lower legs were in the air, waving in time to the song a group of enthusiastic young people were singing on the television.

Kelly shoved paper and crayons to one side of the table. 'Sit down,' she invited Elsie. 'I'll put the kettle on.'

Flipper spotted their visitor. She rolled over, tried to get up too fast, fell over and then tried again. This time she managed to launch herself towards their visitor.

'Hug!' she demanded.

Elsie complied willingly.

'Darn!' Flipper tugged on the older woman's hand.

'Let me catch my breath first, pumpkin,' Elsie begged. 'I had to walk very fast to get here in my lunchbreak.'

'Oh…you're not missing your lunch, are you?' Kelly opened the cupboard over one end of the kitchen bench but it was distressingly bare. A week of not working and buying nothing but the essentials Flipper needed was already making a huge impact. A scary one. 'Can I make you some toast?' she offered apologetically. 'With some baked beans?'

Elsie's face was creased with sympathy. She understood. Kelly was dismayed to find herself suddenly very close to tears. After a week of being so strong, too. Coping. Or was she?

'I brought some sandwiches from the cafeteria,' Elsie said. 'It's nothing exciting, but I couldn't land on your doorstep at lunchtime with nothing in my bag.' She reached into the supermarket carry bag she had placed beside her chair. 'I've got some cake, too. You like cake, don't you, Flipper?'

Flipper stopped turning in circles. 'Cake!' She threw the piece of clown puzzle aside and it hit the screen of the television. Reaching up with her short arms, she tugged at another chair.

'Pick up your toys first,' Kelly instructed. 'And turn off the TV so we can hear ourselves think.'

Flipper ignored her mother. With a frown of determination she tugged harder at the chair and it tipped over backwards, knocking the small girl to the floor and landing on top of her. A frightened wail ensued.

'Oh, no!' Kelly moved swiftly from the kitchen sink. 'Are you hurt?'

'She's fine,' Elsie said. 'It was just a little bump.'

Don't make too much of a fuss, her tone warned. *You'll only blow it all out of proportion and make Flipper think she's hurt herself.*

Kelly froze. She wouldn't normally be rushing to her child like this, would she? She *was* overreacting. Elsie was helping Flipper to her feet and onto her knee, but Flipper was still crying and the sound cut through Kelly like a knife. She'd be crying a whole lot more after she had her surgery, wouldn't she? This was nothing compared to—

'The kettle's overflowing,' Elsie warned.

'Oh, God!' Kelly had forgotten to turn the tap off. Water was pouring over the top of the electric jug and running over the bench to trickle down the cupboard doors and puddle on the floor.

It took a few minutes to sort the mess out. By then Flipper had completely forgotten the bump from the chair. She climbed off Elsie's lap and stood in front of the television, singing loudly and tunelessly along with the song.

Kelly put a mug of tea in front of Elsie and sat down with another sigh.

'Sorry.'

'What about, love?'

'This…' Kelly's hand made a gesture that was intended to cover the mess, the noise of the television and the small upset with Flipper, but she felt as if she was pointing to her entire life. 'I…I thought I was actually coping, you know?'

'You are, love. You have every right to feel stressed. You're worried. How *is* Flipper?'

'I'm watching her too carefully. Reading too much into small things. It's driving us both nuts, I think.'

'It would do you both good to have some time

away from each other. There must be a crèche nearby? Or a playcentre?'

'They cost. And I'm going to have to be really careful until I find a new job.'

'I've written a reference for you. It was one of the reasons I came today.' Elsie's eyes looked suspiciously bright. 'I just wish there was more I could do.'

'Thank you, Elsie. You're a good friend. But you can't fix this. Nobody can.'

'I'll bet your Dr Grimshaw could. It's because of *him* that you got into all this trouble.'

'He's not *my* Dr Grimshaw, Elsie. And he's not going to do anything to try and help.'

Elsie looked offended. 'Why not?'

'Because I told him not to. I said I didn't need him. That I didn't want anything more to do with him.'

Elsie was silent for a moment, searching Kelly's face. 'Oh, my dear! It's not true, is it?'

'Yes. No…' The tears that had been kept at bay successfully for a week now were gathering strength. A single drop escaped and trickled down the side of Kelly's nose. 'It's impossible, Elsie. It could never work.'

'Love can find a way of making all sorts of things work. Oh, love, you *are* in a misery, aren't you?' Elsie put her hand on top of Kelly's and gave it a squeeze.

There were thumping sounds behind Kelly. Flipper was whirling round and round to the music on the children's programme.

Kelly scrubbed at her face and sniffed. 'Things

will get better. I'll make them better. I'll get another
job and find a new crèche for Flipper. I've got all the
paperwork to apply for benefit until then. I just
haven't got round to filling it in. And your reference
will be a help, I'm sure. I—'

Elsie wasn't listening. She had turned her head to
watch Flipper.

Kelly turned as well.

Just in time to see her daughter's strangely blank
expression, and the way her eyes rolled back as she
crumpled and fell to the floor with a dreadful thump.
She just lay there. A tiny and very still shape in the
middle of the rug.

Another chair tipped over backwards as Kelly
made a dive towards Flipper, but it went unnoticed.
Kelly turned the little girl gently onto her back. She
tilted her head to open her airway and then bent over
her, her cheek beside Flipper's nose and mouth and
one hand resting on her chest to feel for air
movement. Her other hand was on a chubby neck,
searching for a carotid pulse.

'She's not breathing,' she whispered in horror,
seconds later. 'There's no pulse! Oh, my God…
Elsie—call an ambulance, please. *Hurry!*'

Kelly bent her head to breathe into Flipper's
mouth and nose. She put her hand in the middle of
the tiny chest and began compressions.

The huge whiteboard in the main corridor of St
Patrick's operating theatre suite was a series of boxes.

Theatre numbers were listed on the left hand side.

The scheduled start time for surgery in that theatre came in the next column, then the names of the surgeons, the procedure being done, and the name and age of the patient. Special details like allergies or MRSA status that could affect protocols could go in the last column.

Tony rubbed at the ache in his neck as he paused to check the start time for his third case of the day. Two p.m. He looked at his watch. Was thirty-five minutes time to snatch a drink and a bite to eat? Check on the latest lab results on that woman on the ward that Josh was concerned about, and check his e-mail to see if there was any word on an announcement regarding the HOD position? Colin Jamieson had put the matter on hold until there was no further threat of any adverse publicity for St Patrick's, but it had been days now. Long, challenging days.

Being this busy was the way he wanted things, however, wasn't it? It was the best way in the world to stop him thinking about anything other than his work.

Mind you, the hurt was wearing off. Had he really been prepared to lose his chance of being HOD for the sake of a relationship? Given the way Kelly had dumped him with such apparent ease, it was just as well he hadn't travelled any further down *that* road.

Yes. There was a good smear of relief at the silver lining of that particular cloud. He was getting good at simply burying such errant thoughts, in any case. An extra glance at his watch did the trick. Sent him straight back to thinking about the afternoon workload. He probably had a little longer than the scheduled time. He would get beeped when the theatre was free of its current case and being set up for the next, and that would give him at least thirty minutes' grace to get back, change into fresh scrubs and scrub up.

The case in Theatre 3 looked complicated, so it could well run over time. The writing in the box for the procedure was tiny to fit it all in. Valve replacements and a heap of other work on a three-year-old girl. Good grief! The name leapt out at him. Philippa Adams.

Flipper?

His gaze flicked to the end column on the right. Yes. Down's Syndrome was recorded as a special detail.

Adams? The child was related to Kelly?

God! It was so easy for his mind to skip. Like a damaged disc or something. It would catch on a memory and replay it until he made the effort to jolt it forward—or, preferably, switch it off.

This time it took him straight back to the night when the things that would send their relationship pear-shaped had been put into place by fate. When the Finch baby had been born.

He remembered the conversation. He could actually *hear* Kelly's voice in his head. Soft and clear and…warm. Saying that one day she would love to have her own baby. To make a family.

And then Tony had to close his eyes for a moment, as another, far more powerful memory superimposed itself. The way he had touched her belly, marvelling at its flat perfection. He could feel her skin now. His fingers actually prickled at the memory of how electric that touch had been.

Jolting his mind forward took a huge effort this time. The glance at his watch was automatic. He was wasting time he couldn't afford to lose. Turning away from the board, Tony strode decisively away. He pushed open the fire stop door, walked a little further, and then stopped dead in his tracks. He was right beside the relatives' waiting area.

The unanswered question was not going to leave him alone, was it? If Kelly was related to that child she would be in there, wouldn't she? Two steps took him to the door of the area. And there, curled into an armchair near a window, staring out with no apparent focus, sat Kelly.

She looked so...so small, curled up like that. Frightened. And alone. Completely alone. There weren't even any other relatives waiting for their cases to finish, to share the space and tension with her. He couldn't leave her like that. She might tell him to go away. He might have to hear once more that she didn't need him or want him. But there was no way he could keep going with the image of her sitting like that on his mind.

He walked quietly into the room. Kelly was obviously waiting for news, because she sensed his approach and turned. The fear in her eyes hit Tony like a physical blow.

'Tony!' Kelly's chest heaved as she drew in a shuddering breath. She licked dry-looking lips. 'I thought it was… *You* haven't come to tell me about Flipper, have you?'

'No. I'm sorry, I don't know how the case is going. Would you like me to go and find out?'

'Yes, please. No!' The catch in her voice made Tony turn back instantly. 'I…'

'Want some company?' Tony held her gaze. He couldn't have looked away, no matter how much he might have wanted to. And he didn't want to. It didn't matter what Kelly had said to him. Her need to have him here with her right now was in her eyes. She needed him, and that was all that mattered.

He sat down beside her. Took hold of her hand.

'What's going on?' he asked gently. 'Do you want to talk about it?'

'How did you know I was here?'

'I saw Flipper's name on the whiteboard.'

'But…' Confusion was added to the mix of fear and misery in her eyes.

Such a deep, dark blue at the moment. And there were deep furrows in her brow that Tony wanted to smooth with his thumb.

'But how did you *know*?' Kelly asked. 'About…'

Nobody could look as Kelly did at that moment unless they cared passionately about the outcome of a life-threatening operation. He'd seen this kind of fear before. In the eyes of parents. It wasn't much of a guess.

'About Flipper being your daughter?'

'Y-yes.'

'I didn't. Oh, Kel. Why didn't you tell me?'

'I…couldn't.'

'But why not?' Tony didn't understand. 'You told me about your family. About the accident. Was that really why you had to leave medical school? Didn't Flipper have more to do with it?'

'It was the same thing.'

Tony didn't jump in with another question. He could sense that Kelly wanted to tell him now. She needed time to collect herself.

Which she did. She took a deep breath and then let it out in a long sigh. She didn't look at Tony, but she did grip his hand tightly.

'My sister Karen was pregnant at the time of the accident. Close to full term. The reason they were all in the car together was because Mum and Dad were taking them shopping. To buy baby stuff, like a really nice pram.' Kelly swallowed audibly. 'Karen was the only one in the car who didn't die at the scene. She arrested in the emergency department, though, and…they couldn't get her back. She was just too badly injured.'

She was holding his hand so tightly Tony's fingers were going numb. He didn't move.

'They did a post-mortem Caesarean. Right there in the department. It was…just terrible.'

'My God, you were *there*?'

Kelly simply nodded. 'I'd been in a tutorial in the orthopaedic department. Just down the corridor.' Her voice wobbled precariously and she struggled for control. 'They gave me Flipper to hold as soon as they'd checked her breathing. I think they already knew there was something wrong, but I was allowed to hold her for a few minutes. While I…while I said goodbye to Karen.'

Not only to Karen. She'd had to say farewell to her entire family.

'That tiny scrap of a baby was all I had left of my family,' Kelly continued in a voice that was no more than a whisper. 'And then I found out that she had major heart problems and would need surgery when she was no more than a few days old.'

Kelly had had to organise and attend multiple funerals. She'd had to add the stress of a baby needing open heart surgery to the horrendous grief she must have been suffering.

God. No wonder he had sensed the enormous strength of this woman.

'I gave up medical school because there was no way I could do justice to raising my niece otherwise.' Kelly looked up and met Tony's gaze steadily. 'I don't regret my choice. I'd do it again in a heartbeat. She's my little girl and I love her to bits. I'd do anything for her. Even—'

Even what? Sacrifice a relationship?

Tony frowned. 'Even what?'

She looked away from him. 'Even if other people see her as being…um…less than perfect.'

'What does it matter what other people think?' His frown deepened. 'Did you think it would make a difference to me? To how I saw you? *Us?*'

'Of course.' Kelly gave her head a tiny shake, as if the question was ridiculous.

And Tony knew that he had his answer. Nothing was as important to Kelly as her child. Her next words confirmed that.

'You have no interest in children, Tony. You're the same as your brother and sister. You have a high-flying career that doesn't leave space in your life for a family. Let alone a family that includes a child with special needs.'

'And that's why you said there was no point? That there never had been?'

Something cold inside Tony was melting. She hadn't told him the truth when she'd said she didn't need him. That she didn't want him.

His career! How many of his relationships had foundered already because of his wonderful career? All of them. But he'd thought things were different with Kelly. The way he could talk to her about his work. Share his passion. And it hadn't really mattered in the past. This was different.

Kelly was different.

'It's not just your career, Tony,' Kelly said quietly, as if she could guess where his thoughts were leading. That he could change something in his life to make it possible to include a family. 'Your family only accepts success. Perfection, preferably. Can you imagine your mother's reaction if she knew you were having a relationship with a woman who had a Down's Syndrome child?'

He could. All too well. The only times Tony had ever felt loved as a child had been when he'd been able to produce evidence of distinction. A prize or a certificate or a silver cup. Kelly was right. His mother would never accept such a child.

But why did that have to be so important? Tony was an adult. The opinions of his parents shouldn't actually matter. Or the opinion of his peers. It was the combination of his background and his career that had been too much for this unexpected diversion his life had taken. The Grimshaw world was one where Kelly and her daughter would never fit. He wouldn't want them to. Because that would make them the same as everybody he'd ever known, and what he loved most about Kelly was how different she was.

No wonder she'd hated being at that reception so much.

No wonder she hadn't told him about Flipper. Her precious daughter.

He tightened the grip on her hand. 'Are you sure you don't want me to go and find out how thing's are going?'

He could feel Kelly flinch. Could feel her gathering new strength. Then she nodded. 'Yes, please.'

'Will you be all right? On your own?'

The faint smile was all the answer he needed. She'd been on her own before, through the worst times in her life. She would be all right.

Tony pulled a mask from the box on the wall outside Theatre 3. He went inside, just far enough to see how things were going. Judging by the atmosphere in here, the lengthy and complicated surgery had gone very well. Tony would have easily picked up the smallest signals from the body language of the paediatric surgeons, and there was no hint of tension.

Parameters being measured, like arterial blood gas and acid-base balance and urine output, were all satisfactory, but he'd arrived at the moment of truth. They were preparing to take Flipper off the bypass machine.

The surgeon was using a syringe to remove all the air that had entered the small heart.

'Clamp can come off,' he said. 'How's her temperature?'

'Coming up nicely.'

Now there was tension in the room. Everybody was waiting to see if defibrillation would be needed to coax the heart to start beating again. Whether the end of this life-threatening procedure would be smooth sailing and the result what they had all spent the last several hours working towards.

'VF', the anaesthetist said quietly, for the benefit of those not leaning over the table with the heart in direct vision. Those people would actually be able to see the uncoordinated movement of the heart. A helpless wriggling that would be fatal if it couldn't be changed.

The anaesthetist's gaze was glued to the monitor. Tony moved a little closer so he could watch the trace. A blip appeared through the squiggle. And then another.

'Here we go,' the anaesthetist said finally, satisfaction in his tone. 'She's in sinus rhythm.'

Within a few minutes Tony was able to leave the

theatre. He ripped off his mask and walked so quickly towards the exit that a nurse gave him a startled glance.

'Is something wrong, Dr Grimshaw?'

'Not at all,' he said, without breaking his stride. 'Quite the opposite.'

Kelly jumped to her feet as though she'd been shot as he entered the waiting area.

'It's almost over,' he said as he walked towards her. 'It's gone really well. She'll be on her way to Recovery very soon and then you'll be able to go and sit with her.'

Tony thought that Kelly might be about to faint. He closed the final distance between them and caught her in his arms. She clung to him, silent sobs racking her body, and all Tony could do was hold her.

And feel…responsible.

Thanks to him, she'd lost her job and her means of supporting a child she'd already sacrificed so much for.

Including him. She did need him, whether she was prepared to admit it or not. She wanted to be with him the same way he wanted to be with her.

Maybe there was no way they could be together again, but it wasn't good enough to leave things like this. Tony had come into her life and had made it harder, and Kelly *so* didn't deserve that.

Somehow he had to try and fix this.

CHAPTER ELEVEN

THE worst was over.

It had to be.

Kelly was far too exhausted to consider any of the potential complications Flipper might still be facing.

She had wrapped herself in the reassurance Tony had given her, and the words from the surgeon a little later had been a ribbon to tie up the most precious gift ever.

'It all went superbly well, Kelly,' he'd told her. 'She's a tough little thing, your daughter. I'm confident she'll bounce right back, and the future's looking very much brighter.'

The time in Recovery had morphed seamlessly into this new vigil that the paediatric intensive care unit represented. Kelly was in a glass-walled cubicle, not far from the main central desk, as much a part of the setting as the bank of monitors and the spaghetti junction of tubing and wires surrounding Flipper's bed.

A nurse brought a figure, gowned and masked, to the door of the cubicle.

'I'm only allowed to stay for a minute or two,' Elsie whispered, clearly overawed by her surroundings. 'I told them I was family.'

Kelly looked up from where she was sitting, holding Flipper's hand, and smiled. 'You *are* family, Elsie.' She kept her voice low as well. Not that it was going to disturb Flipper, but there were other parents nearby keeping watch on their critically ill children. 'I couldn't have got through the last few days without you.'

Elsie made a snuffling noise behind the mask, but she didn't step any closer. 'I've brought your clean undies. And those DVDs for Flipper. But I still can't find that frog toy.'

'Oh…' Kelly's heart sank.

It had been three days now since Elsie had come for lunch and ended up being part of that dreadful emergency with Flipper. Elsie had been back to the house several times since, to get whatever Kelly needed so that she didn't have to leave Flipper's bedside, and every time she had conducted a search for Ribby the frog. Flipper had been tearfully begging for the toy ever since that miraculous moment when she'd started breathing for herself again, and had opened her eyes and recognised her mother.

'Did you check at the bottom of her bed? Under the sheets?'

'Yes. And under the couch cushions and in the cupboards. He's vanished. I'm sorry, Kelly.'

'Don't be. You've been a rock. I'll be able to slip home myself before too long. In a day or two, I should think. Maybe a fresh pair of eyes will spot something.'

For a moment both women were silent. The sound of the monitors beeping and the rhythmic hiss of Flipper's breathing, currently controlled by a ventilator, filled the small space.

'Poor wee mite,' Elsie murmured, her voice catching.

'She's doing really well.' Kelly stroked a few strands of hair from Flipper's forehead with her free hand. Her other hand still hadn't moved from where it was curled gently over Flipper's. 'Her cardiac output's better than it's ever been and her blood pressure's normal. Kidney function is good, and her oxygen levels are perfect.'

Elsie's frown showed the medical terminology meant little. 'Has she woken up yet?'

'She's still sedated. They'll lighten it tomorrow, and if she keeps this up she'll be back on the ward in a day or two. It's amazing the way kids can get over this sort of thing.'

'That's good to hear,' Elsie nodded. 'I'd better go, love. That nurse is staring at me. Unless you'd like me to sit with Flipper for a while, so you can get some sleep?'

Kelly shook her head. 'I'm good.'

'You look done in.'

'I am, but I'm still good. There's no way I'm leaving her, Elsie. Not yet.'

When Elsie had gone, and many more quiet minutes had ticked past, Kelly stroked Flipper's forehead again. And again. A feather-light touch. A movement that spoke of exhaustion and relief. Of a mind-numbing state that didn't allow for conscious direction of thought.

Instead, Kelly found herself thinking in snatches of the rollercoaster her life had been over the last few weeks.

When had she stepped onto that wild ride?

When she'd purchased the raffle ticket for entrance to the ball?

Or had it been the ball itself? That moment when she'd seen Tony watching her from between the pillars and she'd been dancing. For *him*.

That had certainly been the start of the upward sweep.

Rediscovering the joy of dancing. Learning for the first time what it was like to really fall in love.

There had been smaller dips. Like meeting Tony's parents and knowing that she could never fit into his kind of world. That conversation about babies and realising that a family didn't fit into Tony's future. The results of Flipper's tests and the worry that had come in their wake.

Losing her job had to have been the stomach curdling moment when she'd known the downward rush was just about to begin.

Then rock bottom. When Flipper had collapsed and Kelly had thought she'd lost her.

And now?

Now it felt like an upward roll again. One that had begun when Tony had been holding her as she sobbed out the relief of hearing that Flipper's surgery had been a success.

And here she was, touching her little girl. Feeling her warmth. Watching the rise and fall of her small chest with every breath. Hearing the reassuring soft beeps of the monitors.

It was all she could ask for right now.

All she wanted.

It was late.

The longest day in the longest week of Tony Grimshaw's life, but he couldn't go home just yet.

He went to the paediatric intensive care unit instead.

To the central desk, to find which of the dimly lit cubicles Kelly and Flipper would be in. He'd spoken to the surgeon not so long ago, so he knew how well Flipper was doing. It wasn't enough to hear that Kelly was also coping well. He needed to see for himself.

The nursing staff were quietly occupied elsewhere, but Tony didn't need to ask or even check the list he knew would be on the desk somewhere. As soon as he reached the central area he could see her, straight ahead of him.

His forward movement ceased and Tony simply stood there for a minute, his gaze riveted on the scene in that cubicle.

Kelly was sitting beside the bed but her body was tilted inwards, almost curling over the tiny girl to offer protection. He could see her brushing back Flipper's hair. Again and again.

So softly.

A gentle touch he knew so well he could feel it himself as he watched.

But what really transfixed him, brought a lump to his throat and actually threatened to bring tears to his eyes for the first time in living memory, was the expression on Kelly's face.

Fierce, pure love.

The kind that would let nothing and no one harm the beloved if it was within human power to offer protection.

The kind that Tony hadn't really believed existed outside a fairytale. Not like this. Not when someone had chosen to bestow it, despite obstacles that would have turned many people away.

It was partly the physical problems Flipper had, partly that she was a special needs child, but mostly Tony could relate to the fact that Kelly had sacrificed her career to bestow this love.

He knew so well the passion and dedication it took to become a doctor. His parents had both had careers. Would his mother have considered *him* more important as a baby than her law practice? Would his father have given up his political aspirations?

No. Tony had never been loved like this.

Flipper had to be the luckiest little girl in existence. Even with everything she had been through and was going through now, she had experienced that kind of love. The best that life could offer anyone. Celebrations in her life would be with home-cooked food prepared with love. Not in a fancy restaurant where no more effort was required than making a choice from a menu. Where someone else dealt with the mess. Tony knew what was real. He knew what he would have chosen for the child that had been himself.

And it was too late.

Or was it?

It beggared belief that Kelly could love her daughter this much and still have the same kind of love to offer someone else, but he knew she did. He could hear her voice again, softly expressing her wish for a family. To have a baby with someone who loved her as much as she loved him.

Someone who would be the luckiest man in the world. Someone who hadn't been programmed to think that what mattered in life was success. Public accolade.

It took a moment or two to recognise the ugly feeling that the thought of that person generated.

Someone other than himself being loved by Kelly.

Making love to her.

Making a baby.

Jealousy. That was what it was.

The idea was so abhorrent. It was unacceptable. It couldn't happen. Tony wasn't going to allow it to happen.

Somehow he would have to convince Kelly that they could make it work. But not right now. He couldn't disturb her. The bond with her daughter was too tight at the moment. And too important.

The rest of his life was at stake here. Being patient for a day or two was a small price to pay if it was going to improve the odds.

'You've just missed her, I'm afraid.' The nurse's badge was a bright flower, with "Jo" written in the centre.

'When will she be back?'

'Not for a little while. She's gone home to find a toy that Flipper's been begging for.'

'Ribby!' said the small girl in the cot.

Tony smiled. 'Ribby?'

He was rewarded with the grin of a pixie.

'Ribby's the name of the toy,' Jo explained. 'I believe it's a frog, and it's been lost for a few days.'

Tony nodded, but he was still looking at the small face. The way this little girl was standing up and hanging onto the top rail of the cot with such a determined grip. It was only three days since her surgery. 'She's doing well, isn't she?'

'She's fabulous.' Jo leaned over and ruffled Flipper's hair. 'Aren't you, tuppence?'

'Darn!' Flipper held up both arms.

Jo laughed. 'You'll be dancing again soon enough, pet.'

Tony found himself stepping closer. 'You like to dance, Flipper? Your mummy likes to dance too, doesn't she?'

Flipper was holding his eye contact. Smiling so hard her face was a mass of crinkles. She nodded, and moved along the cot like a crab, holding on with only one hand. The other hand was stretching towards Tony.

'Darn!' she commanded.

'You can't run around yet,' Jo reminded her. 'How about I put on one of your DVDs? Or read you a story?'

Flipper shook her head. Her grin was fading rapidly and her bottom lip quivered.

'Is she allowed to be picked up?'

The nurse gave him an astonished look.

'I like dancing myself,' Tony said with a grin. 'Maybe…'

Jo sucked in a breath. 'It's OK to pick her up, and if anyone knows what they're doing I'm sure you do, Dr Grimshaw. But—'

'I'll be gentle,' Tony promised. 'And quick. We don't want tears, do we?'

Without giving the nurse time to argue, Tony leaned over the cot and found two chubby arms wound trustingly around his neck. He held the child with one arm, and with the other he kept the IV pole close. He stepped back, then forward, then turned in a small circle.

'See?' He smiled at Jo. 'Dancing!'

'Faster!' Flipper said. She thumped Tony on his back.

There was a new spring in Kelly's step today.

It was only a week since Flipper's surgery, and she was doing so well they were talking about letting her come home.

And Kelly had a new job. Flipper's nurse, Jo, had thought of it. She had a friend who worked in an old people's home that happened to have a crèche right next door. It was quite a long way from where they lived, but they could catch the bus every day and it might even be fun.

Jo had been so excited when she'd arrived at the hospital this morning. She'd seen her friend the night before, and apparently they were looking for a new staff member at the home. So Kelly had dashed out this afternoon and gone for an interview and they'd loved her. She didn't have to start right away. Not until Flipper was ready to go to the crèche. It was perfect.

A short detour into a corner shop was made, so that Kelly could buy some of the jelly snakes that were Flipper's favourite treat. Having made the purchase, she found a sense of urgency in getting back to the hospital and picked up the speed of her walk. Not that Flipper would be missing her unduly. She was having a ball on the ward. Other children were drawn to her friendly grin, and the staff could never resist the freely given cuddles. Every day her condition had improved noticeably—to the point where it was getting hard to keep her anywhere near her bed. Both the surgeon and Dr Clifford had laughed about it this morning.

'Time to think about sending her home, I think,' the surgeon had said. 'Are you happy with that, Kelly?'

Happy? She couldn't get any happier.

With the little bag of jelly snakes clutched in her hand, Kelly sped through the hospital corridors towards the paediatric ward. Flipper's room was near the entrance to the ward, but she wasn't a bit surprised to find it empty. Flipper would be down in the playroom, probably, with the other children. She turned to go in that direction, down the wide corridor.

It was late in the afternoon now. Sunshine poured in through this side of the building at this time of day, so the figure down at the end of the corridor was a dark shape. An oddly lumpy shape, that was moving in a very peculiar fashion.

Stepping forwards and backwards rapidly. Spinning. *Dancing!*

The peal of childish laughter was instantly recognisable. Someone was whirling around with Flipper in their arms. Spinning and—dear Lord—dipping now. Holding her precious little girl sideways, with her head almost touching the floor.

Kelly's heart missed a beat, and then kicked in at a ferocious speed. Her feet picked up the same rhythm as she hurtled down the corridor to rescue her daughter. But then the speed ebbed as fast as she'd turned it on. Her jaw dropped and she came to a complete halt.

The person dancing with Flipper was *Tony!*

And he wasn't just dancing the way you might with a small child, with token moves and a lot of laughter. He was seriously dancing with her. As though he was enjoying it. As though it *mattered.*

Kelly knew what it was like to be held like that. To have Tony so focussed on holding her. To feel the sweep of movement and the beat of his heart. Not that there was any music happening here.

So why was her heart singing?

Why did this, more than any of the joy of watching Flipper's rapid recovery over the last week or so, make her throat close up and tears sting the back of her eyes.

'Mummy!'

Flipper had spotted her. Tony stopped the dance abruptly and bent to let the small, wriggling person escape his hold. She ran to Kelly and wrapped her arms around her mother's knees.

'Darn, Mummy!'

'You *were* dancing, darling. I saw you.'

But Kelly wasn't looking down at Flipper as she spoke. Her gaze was caught by the man in front of her. By the expression in his eyes. He looked...hopeful? Was he expecting her to be angry at the level of physical activity he had been encouraging? Or the fact that he was dancing with her daughter?

Kelly had to clear her throat. She rested her hand on the top of Flipper's head. 'It was beautiful dancing,' she said softly.

'Wasn't it just?' Jo appeared from the shadows further down the corridor. 'She's come along a treat in her dance lessons in the last few days.'

'Few days?' Kelly's eyebrows shot up. 'You've been doing this for *days*?'

'We're dance partners,' Tony admitted. There was a faint upward tilt to the corners of his mouth. 'Only because you weren't here.'

Kelly was really confused now. 'You came here to *dance* with me?'

Flipper had bent her head backwards so she could stare up at Kelly without letting go of her legs. 'Darn, Mummy?'

'I came here to *talk* to you,' Tony said. 'But you weren't here. You'd gone home to get Ribby. He was lost, wasn't he? Where did you find him?'

This was so weird. Hearing Tony say that ridiculous name as though it was perfectly ordinary. The man who had no interest in children. In families. Talking about a fluffy toy as though it was important.

'He was in the washing machine,' Kelly said cautiously. 'I think Flipper thought Ribby needed a bath—didn't you, sweetie?'

'Ribby!' Flipper repeated happily. She let go of Kelly's legs. 'Wanna play with Ribby.'

She trotted off and disappeared into her room.

Kelly stared at Tony, a curious bubbling sensation happening deep inside. 'You wanted to talk to me?'

He nodded. 'I kept coming back. I always seemed to miss you.' His gaze held hers as it softened. 'I *do* miss you, Kelly. Too much.'

Jo's jaw dropped. 'I'd better go and see what Flipper's up to,' she said hurriedly. 'And the dinner trolley's going to be arriving any minute.'

'I miss you, too,' Kelly said softly. 'I've been hoping I'd see you.'

'You have?'

'Mmm. I wanted to thank you for being with me the day of the surgery. It was a…a very special thing to do.'

'I wanted to be there,' Tony said. 'I want to be with you, Kelly.'

'But…'

She didn't get time to articulate why it wasn't a good idea. Why they'd both end up getting hurt if they tried something that had no hope of working out. Flipper was back. Ribby the frog dangled from one hand. She stopped and looked up at Tony. Then she looked up at Kelly.

'Darn?' she asked hopefully. Her mouth widened in a confident smile that brought the prickle of tears back to Kelly's eyes. Thank God she was this happy. This healthy now.

'Sure.' Kelly reached down. 'I'll dance with you.'

'No.' Flipper pushed Kelly away. '*You* darn.'

She grinned up at Tony. When neither of the adults moved, she marched forward, took hold of Tony's thumb and dragged him towards Kelly. She dropped Ribby so she could also take hold of Kelly's hand, and then she pulled both the much larger hands together.

'Darn,' she commanded, clearly satisfied that she had sorted the matter.

'Your daughter wants us to dance,' Tony murmured. 'With each other.'

'Mmm.' Kelly's fingers were curled loosely inside Tony's palm. She could feel his fingers moving.

Taking hold of hers. She could feel that grip tighten around her heart as much as her hand.

'Shall we?'

Kelly turned by way of response. So that she was facing Tony and they were only inches apart. She lifted her free hand and put it on his shoulder. He stepped in so that their bodies were touching.

And then he started moving. Leading her in a dance. A slow kind of tango, where their heads stayed close enough for a quiet conversation to continue.

Now was the time to say something. Before she was sucked into this feeling of completeness so deeply it would be impossible to say anything to end it.

'It could never work, Tony. Everybody knows that I was a nurse aide. Pretty much the same thing as being a cleaner. You'd never live it down.'

Tony dipped her. He leaned over her with his face just above hers. 'And you think that what you do is what really matters?'

Flipper hooted with glee. 'More!' she shouted.

'It's who you are that's important to me,' Tony said as he lifted her upright again. 'The woman I love is strong and independent and loving. She's the most amazing woman I've ever met. Or ever will.'

He *loved* her?

The wave of sensation was so intense it made Kelly's head spin, so she rested it on Tony's shoulder. It didn't matter that they had no music to dance to. They could still keep a perfect rhythm.

Flipper was holding Ribby by his fluffy front legs. She was dancing beside them and singing tunelessly. Dancing with her toy in her own little happy world.

A world that couldn't be allowed to be tarnished.

'Can you imagine Flipper living in your home?' she asked Tony quietly. 'Singing and dancing like this when you've got some kind of reception you have to hold as Head of Department?'

'I'm not the head of department. I never will be. Well, maybe in twenty or thirty years, when I don't have more important things to keep me busy.'

'What?' Kelly lifted her head. 'But—'

Tony grinned, swirling her in a circle. 'I pulled out of contention,' he told her. 'I realised where I'd gone wrong. *You* made me realise.'

He gave her a series of swirls that made Flipper laugh in delight, but Kelly was feeling alarmed. He'd given up wanting to be HOD because of *her*?

'My life has been one long series of ambitions,' Tony said, pulling her close again and slowing the dance. Moving her to one side of the corridor to let the dinner trolley get past. 'One goal after another. I've chased them and I've caught them, but they've never been enough—and do you know why?'

'No,' Kelly whispered.

'They've been the wrong goals. I never knew what the most important goal of all was until I met you. Until I saw you with Flipper.'

Some more children had joined Flipper.

'What are they doing?' one of them asked.

'Darn—sing,' Flipper enunciated proudly.

'Cool.' The children lined up to watch.

'What's Flipper got to do with *us*?' Kelly asked in wonder.

'Everything.'

That was the right answer. Kelly could feel her smile starting. Growing.

'She's the luckiest little girl in the world, being loved so much.' Tony sent her out, made her spin around, then drew her back so fast she landed against his body with a soft thump. 'More particularly because she's loved by *you*.'

Kelly caught her breath. Tony could be too, if that was what he wanted.

He *looked* as though that was what he wanted.

She wanted to tell him. She wanted to stop moving just for a moment, so she could find the right words to tell him how much she loved him. But there was movement everywhere. All the children who had been watching were dancing now as well. Even a boy on crutches was hopping in small circles.

'Dinnertime!' Jo's cheerful call cut into Kelly's whirling thoughts. 'Or are you lot planning to dance all night?'

'I wish,' Tony muttered. But he let Kelly go. 'Flipper needs you.'

So do you, Kelly wanted to say. *We need each other. All of us.*

But Tony was turning to leave. Then he turned again. To wave at Flipper and smile at Kelly.

'I'll be back,' he promised. 'Later.'

* * *

How late was 'later'?

Flipper had been asleep for hours now. Ten p.m. came and went. Eleven. The minutes ticked past and Kelly tried to stop herself watching the door.

Waiting.

He'd promised he'd come back and he would. The trust was there.

The hope.

As the figures on her watch changed to show midnight, Kelly became aware of an odd sound.

A kind of swishing outside the door.

She got up and peered into the dimly lit corridor. A janitor was mopping the floor.

Disappointment coursed through her so intense she just stood there for a few seconds, watching the mop as it swept in arcs that brought it closer and closer to her door.

And then the janitor in the stained grey coat looked up, and Kelly gasped.

'Oh, my God! *Tony!*'

He grinned.

'What on earth are you doing?'

'Cleaning.'

'Why?'

Tony propped the mop back into the bucket. He stepped towards Kelly and took hold of both her hands.

'Because I love you, Kelly Adams, and I couldn't think of a better way to show you.'

'By mopping the floor? I don't understand.'

'It's about who we are, not what we do,' Tony told

her quietly. 'It's about being real. Cleaning floors seems pretty real.'

'What if someone had seen you?'

'Someone *did* see me.'

'Oh, no! Who?'

'You.'

Kelly gave a soft huff. 'But that's not embarrassing. I don't matter.'

'On the contrary.' Tony's thumbs made circles on the backs of Kelly's hands. 'You matter more than anyone else could ever hope to. Except maybe my other dance partner. The short one. Is she asleep?'

'Yes. With Ribby clutched in her arms, of course.'

'Ah. The frog prince.' Tony smiled, and suddenly Kelly understood.

'You're doing this because of the way we met?' Kelly bit her lip, not quite ready to release the bubble of joy inside her in the form of a smile. 'The Cinderella thing?'

'Yes. I know it's the wrong way round, and I'm not the one who should be doing the cleaning—but, hey, I'm no prince either. I'm nowhere near perfect enough.'

The smile began to escape. He was perfect enough for *her*.

'What I am is a bit older and wiser than I've ever been before,' Tony continued. 'And I have to thank you for teaching me something I might never have learned otherwise. For teaching me about love.'

The look on Tony's face was so tender it made Kelly want to cry. Her smile wobbled.

'I think I fell in love with you the first time I saw you,' Tony said. 'I fell in love with a princess.'

'I'm no princess.'

But Tony didn't seem to be listening. He had let go of her hands and was fishing in the pocket of the horrible grey coat he was wearing. 'I know this is all inside out and upside down, but I really wanted to do this.' He pulled something out of his pocket. 'It's the slipper,' he said sombrely. 'And I'm really hoping it fits.'

Kelly's laugh was a gurgle of pure joy.

'It's a disposable theatre bootee,' she whispered. 'It would fit anyone.'

'But it's you I want it to fit.' Tony dropped to one knee and touched her foot. 'Will you try it on?'

Kelly just smiled down at him. 'I love you, Tony Grimshaw.'

He stayed on his knee. He fished inside the bootee. 'If you won't try the shoe on,' he said, 'could you see if this fits instead?'

'*Oh!*'

Tony was holding a ring. A simple, solitaire diamond ring that could only mean one thing.

The intensity of what she was feeling made Kelly's knees distinctly wobbly. She sank down. And there she was, kneeling on the floor in front of Tony.

'I love you,' he said softly. 'More than I can ever say, but I'm going to keep trying. Every day for as long as I live. If you'll let me.'

'Oh…' Kelly still couldn't find any words. She

held out her hand, aware of the moisture on her cheeks as Tony slid the ring onto her finger.

'Will you marry me?' he asked. 'And dance with me and clean floors with me? Now and for ever?'

'Yes,' Kelly managed. 'Oh, *Tony!*'

He kissed her. A long, tender kiss that made her tears fall even faster. Tears of joy. He kissed her again, and then brushed her cheeks with his thumbs. 'Don't move,' he smiled. 'I think I'd better get my mop.'